GIV
THE

Also by Max McCoy

Of Grave Concern

The Spirit Is Willing

GIVING UP THE GHOST

MAX MCCOY

KENSINGTON PUBLISHING CORP.
http://www.kensingtonbooks.com

KENSINGTON BOOKS are published by

Kensington Publishing Corp.
119 West 40th Street
New York, NY 10018

All Kensington Titles, Imprints, and Distributed Lines are available at special quantity discounts for bulk purchases for sales promotions, premiums, fund-raising, and educational or institutional use. Special book excerpts or customized printings can also be created to fit specific needs. For details, write or phone the office of the Kensington special sales manager: Kensington Publishing Corp., 119 West 40th Street, New York, NY 10018, attn: Special Sales Department, Phone: 1-800-221-2647.

Kensington and the K logo Reg. U.S. Pat & TM Off.

ISBN-13: 978-0-7582-8197-5
ISBN-10: 0-7582-8197-8
First Kensington Mass Market Edition: December 2015

eISBN-13: 978-0-7582-8198-2
eISBN-10: 0-7582-8198-6
First Kensington Electronic Edition: December 2015

10 9 8 7 6 5 4 3 2 1

Printed in the United States of America

Dodge City has a very hard name in the East, and that "Boot Hill," our graveyard, is considered almost as great a curiosity as the grave of Shakespeare. Mr. Ludwig (a visitor from the East) selected some small pebbles from "Boot Hill," and will carry them home and put them in a vase and place the vase on his parlor center table, as a constant reminder of the renowned graveyard of the far West.

—*Dodge City Times,* 1877

It takes a thousand men to invent a telegraph, or a steam engine, or a phonograph, or a photograph, or a telephone, or any other important thing—and the last man gets the credit and we forget the others.

—Mark Twain, *Letters*

1

Consider your death, whispered the voice in my head. *You are a stem of dry grass broken on the endless prairie, a star fallen from the lower lights to the unforgiving earth, a sparrow trapped in the chimney of an abandoned house.*

I turned away from my friend and, with a gloved hand, brushed away the tears scalding my cheeks. Hating myself for my weakness, I smiled and mumbled some excuse about the cold.

"*Cré nom,*" I cursed. "Now I know why it is called the dead of winter."

"But how still is the air, and soundless," Doc McCarty said. "So like a dream."

McCarty knelt beside a mound of dirt, heedless of his trousers, watching as a hired man steadily increased the pile one shovelful at a time on a newly opened grave. The man sang as he worked, a popular tune that the cowboys favored in the bars that lined both sides of Front Street.

"*Oh!*" the hired man cried. "*Give me a gale of the*

*Solomon vale, where the life streams with buoyancy
flow."*

The man's diction was wretched, for he sang
with a cheek full of tobacco, but I had heard the
tune often enough to know the words. I had no
idea where the Solomon valley might be, or why
a pleasant wind should blow there, and I had
even less of a notion of what magic "life streams"
might burble. But it all sounded pleasant enough,
even if the song itself was wretched.

It was a Sunday in January, a week after Old
Christmas.

The sky was a deepening shade of blue, and
the evening star had already appeared as hard
and bright as a diamond in the west. The ground
was frozen, and the hired man had earlier built
bonfires over the graves, and spread the glowing
coals, to thaw the earth. Still, he had been forced
to use a pickax to break the top few inches. The
work had been commissioned six months before,
in the stifling heat of summer, but the exhuma-
tions were delayed until the cold might serve
some sanitary measure.

From our perch on Boot Hill, we had a good
view of Dodge City, dull and drowsy now that the
cattle season was long over. The last time I had
stood on this spot, more than a year before, there
was plenty of room between the cemetery and
the town; now I could have hit the nearest building with a not too vigorously thrown rock.

A train was at the depot, headed west, crouching toward Colorado. Black smoke curled from

its stack and steam gushed from its belly, while it took on water from the tank. Behind the hulking locomotive and its companion tender was a line of cars painted an impatient yellow.

In every other direction the sea of wheat-colored grass on the dormant prairie rustled in the chilling wind, a reminder that to every life winter must come. I pulled my coat tightly around me and turned my back to the wind, but it made me no warmer.

Then the hired man's singing stopped, in the middle of a line about discouraging words. He handed up an object to McCarty.

It was a skull, as white as the natural keys of the piano in the Saratoga Saloon, but caked with the red clay of Boot Hill.

"Who have we here?" McCarty asked.

The hired man said he didn't know, for the grave was unmarked.

"Judging from the roundness, the density of the bone, and the smoothness of the brow ridge—a woman," McCarty said. "Even in death, the fair sex retains a certain grace."

"How old was she?" I asked.

"Thirty years or so."

That was my age.

"May I hold her?" I asked.

"Is that wise?" McCarty asked.

"Considering my temporary burial in Boot Hill, some seasons past? I have come to terms with that unpleasantness. Besides, I would like to regard our ultimate transformation. Hand her over, and gently."

McCarty passed me the skull, and I was surprised at how light it was. I ran my fingers over the bone, peered into the eye sockets, and traced with my fingers the serpentine channels where pulsating rivulets of blood—those living streams where buoyancy truly flows—had once stoked the thinking and feeling brain inside.

"Who are you?" I asked.

Doc McCarty grew still and the hired hand leaned on the shaft of his shovel, watching, hoping, I think, for me to receive some otherworldly intelligence from the orb in my hands. But there was nary a whisper. Her name may have been unknown to us, but the owner of the skull was among the peaceful dead, having crossed over with no unfinished business behind.

I handed the skull back to McCarty.

"She is a mystery," I said.

"A whore, most likely," the hired man said, and spat into the grave.

I cast my best frown upon him.

"If so, no longer," McCarty said, using his thumb to brush away a clod of dirt from an ivory cheekbone. "The grave has removed every stain of flesh."

The hired man spat again, harder.

McCarty smiled his knowing, gentle smile.

"'Is she to be buried in Christian burial that willfully seeks her own salvation?'" McCarty quoted, turning his soft blue eyes toward me. Then he answered, playing the part of the other grave-digging clown from *Hamlet* as well. "'I tell thee she is, and therefore make her grave straight: the crowner hath sate on her, and finds it Christian burial.'"

"You talk nonsense," the hired man said. "A crowner sitting on a corpse."

"A crowner is a coroner," McCarty said. "At least it was in Shakespeare's time. Then, as now, a coroner is an official charged with inquests into the deaths of those who may have died by accident or violence, including self-slaughter— and for judging ownership of a treasure trove."

"Treasure," the hired man snorted, then wiped tobacco spittle from his chin with the back of a dirty hand. "No buried treasure here, just bones."

"All the same," McCarty said. "I am the crowner here and declare her death blameless. I bid you make her new grave straight."

The man slowly shook his head.

"Colonel Straughn is the coroner," he said. "And a deputy sheriff for Ford County. The town council gave him the contract for the removals, and he hired me for the work, seeing as how he is in the Colorado gold fields."

"The fact that the work is a mite unpleasant may have had something to do with it as well," McCarty said. "I understand John Straughn is the coroner, and I am merely an assistant. I was making a literary point, my friend."

The hired man scratched his head.

"'Cudgel thy brains no more,'" McCarty said.

"Lunatics," he said. "A mad doctor and a . . ."

I looked at him expectantly and his voice trailed off.

"Go on," I said. "How were you going to describe me?"

His reply was inaudible.

"I'm sorry, I couldn't make that out," I said. "Were you describing me as perhaps another member of the Cyprian sisterhood?"

"No, girl," the hired man said. "I was saying how I was afraid of you."

The answer took me by surprise.

"What have I done?"

"Nothing. Not to me," the hired man said. "But I hear folks talk."

"What do they say?"

"Pay him no mind," McCarty urged.

"No, I'd like to hear it."

I asked the hired man his name.

"Decker."

"Well, Decker. You needn't be afraid. Tell me."

"They say you're a witch."

I took this in for a moment.

"Is that all?"

"The way you dress," he said. "It's a puzzle."

I smiled.

"You are kind for telling me," I said.

He gave a shrug, then turned back to his work.

"It's late," McCarty said, glancing at the darkening sky. Then he placed the skull in a wooden box, along with some other bones. Around us there were dozens of other open graves, where the hill had reluctantly given up its dead. The bones and crumbling coffins and sometimes mummified remains with crossed boots as pillows were being removed to a new cemetery, a patch of consecrated ground a half mile northeast of town, a somber garden surrounded by a white wooden fence and which had rows and walkways and where burial plots sold for five dollars each. The new cemetery was called Prairie Grove, although there were no trees.

It was the end of Boot Hill.

The idea made me feel peculiar, because in newspapers across the country the ramshackle little cemetery had come to represent Dodge City—the wildest and most wicked and undoubtedly the weirdest town in the West. We had climbed the hill on that cold winter afternoon to say good-bye to Boot Hill and its inhabitants, a move forced by the town council to make way for new homes.

Doc McCarty and I were the only mourners.

Decker, the hired man, began singing that bloody song again.

"Home, home on the range."

The deer and antelope played, there was never a discouraging word, and the skies were not cloudy all day.

My dark inner voice immediately spun back the lyrics.

Oh! Give me a home, where the dead do not roam
With the ghosts and the demons at bay
Where never is heard an ethereal word
And to die is the end of the play!

"Can't you sing something different?" I asked. "Something less cloyingly cheerful?"

And harder to parody, I added silently.

Decker leaned on the handle of his spade and stared stupidly at me.

"I like the song," he said.

"That doesn't mean you should infect the rest of us with it."

McCarty gave me a disapproving look.

"Pardon," I said. "But it's a horrible song. I don't think the person who wrote it has ever been here. This is the edge of the world; the summers are hellish, the winters are brutal, and the damned wind never stops blowing. The only governing principles of human behavior here seem to be the seven deadlies, with assorted venials thrown in for good measure."

Decker sighed.

"Not to worry," McCarty said. "We must be leaving."

My friend stood, then attempted to brush the clay from his knees.

"You've ruined another pair of Montgomery Wards," I observed.

McCarty cursed.

"What do you want me to do with the other one?" Decker asked.

"The other *what*?" McCarty asked, still swatting at his knees.

"The other pumpkin," Decker said. "Kalamazoo Charley. The one that has been ventilated right here."

Decker tapped his left temple.

"Oh, I almost forgot about him," McCarty said. "Bring the skull to my office, won't you?"

"You're not going to keep it, are you?" I asked.

"What's a doctor's office without a grinning skull sitting on the desk, especially an interesting one with a bullet hole?" McCarty said. "No, my dear, I'm not going to keep it; my interest is strictly academic, and Kalamazoo Charley's head will be rejoined with the rest of his bones once my examination is complete."

"It still seems morbid," I said.

"It's not morbid," McCarty said. "It's science. Come, let us get you home. To warmth."

"That's the loveliest thought I've heard today."

He offered his arm and I took it.

"Why so melancholy?" McCarty asked as we walked down the hill. "Is your last adventure troubling you?"

"Why, Doc," I said. "You're not as oblivious as you seem. And, I should remind you, it was *our* adventure."

The Case of the Electro-Magnetic Revenant?

"I haven't decided on a title."

"Not to your liking?"

"Sounds like a patent application. I was thinking of something along the lines of *The Ghost in the Wire*. But I'm sure my publisher, Mr. Garrick Sloane of Boston, will have his own ideas about the title—and choose something that conjures a warm, rather than frightening, image, as he did with my first two modest efforts. In any event, the case is properly resolved, and all that is left is to put it to paper."

"So it is not the case that vexes you," McCarty said. "Has something transpired lately to cause some private agony?"

"All the best agonies are private ones."

"Confide in me, Ophie."

I paused, and because our arms were looped, this caused McCarty to stop as well. He searched my face with those bright eyes, and I looked upon that familiar face beneath the shock of boyish hair, and I softened a bit. If there was one person I could trust with a secret, it was Doc. He was the closest thing to kin I had in the world, and I loved him as I would a favorite uncle.

"Tom," I said. "I have been reflecting of late on morbid things."

"That is your line of work."

"No," I said. "I have been dwelling on intensely personal morbid things. My own mental voice has become a stranger to me, whispering the worst thoughts. As if my own soul mocks me."

"This isn't some kind of possession?"

"Not at all," I said. "It is, sadly, me—but the darkest and most hopeless version of me, and driven as mad as my namesake."

"Do you feel this darkest of Ophelias is urging you to—"

"Drown myself in the Arkansas?"

McCarty paused before replying.

"Yes," he said.

"No."

"There are other ways of breaking the mortal coil," he said.

"I dislike guns."

"You have a fierce imagination," McCarty said. "There are innumerable substitutes. Besides, women seldom commit the act with a firearm. They are most likely to use poison, in my experience."

McCarty slipped a hand into his vest pocket. He emerged with a pale, cubelike stone in the fingers of his right hand, a stone about the size of a die used in a game of craps.

"Take it."

I took the cube and weighed it in my gloved palm. It was roughly hewn, showing chisel marks on all sides but one. That side was strangely polished.

"It's a sort of good luck," McCarty said. "Something I've carried for many years. It is Jerusalem limestone, cut from one of the paving stones from the Via Dolorosa. It is among the few things left today that we can be reasonably sure was touched by our Savior."

"Does the bottom of His sandal count?"

McCarty did not laugh.

"He fell many times beneath the burden of the cross, and his hands and knees—and perhaps even his blood—may have contacted the stone. I brought it back with me from a tour of the Holy Land before the war. It has given me surprising comfort in times of need."

"Doc, I thought you were a scientist."

"Look at the face of stone," he said. "It has been polished smooth by the passage of countless feet over the centuries. Even if Christ did not touch the stone—or even if His divinity were not greater than ours—it gives me comfort to know that so many have gone before us, and that each generation pushed us a little closer to the light of truth, both scientific and spiritual."

"Doc, some of those generations shoved us back," I said. "It was called the Dark Ages for a reason. And it wasn't so long ago that we were burning women who were suspected of witchcraft at the stake."

I held out my hand for him to take it back, but he shook his head.

"You're the one who brought it back," I said. "You have the sentimental attachment. It belongs to you."

"Keep it," Doc said. "For me, at least for a little while. Carry it on your person. And when you feel a need for comfort, close your hand around it, and if it doesn't please you to think of Christ, reflect at least upon the affection of the friend who gave it to you."

I slipped the stone in my pocket and began again to cry.

Doc offered me his kerchief.

"You're right. Something did happen, between the end of the case and our return to Dodge City," I said, hating the sound I made when trying to speak while crying. "Something that upended my understanding of what was real, yet in review I should have known all along. It has made me feel the biggest fool in the world. My life is built upon a lie."

McCarty put his arm around my shoulders.

"What was it?" he asked.

"I cannot say," I said, and again the tears came. "It mortifies me just to think upon it. If you were not holding me up, my knees would buckle and I would sink to the ground, and I do not think I could ever get up again."

"Only love can lay one so low."

I did not answer.

"What about Jack Calder?" he asked. "This is surely something you should speak to him about. As your partner in detection, if not affection."

"Calder," I said sharply. "Calder of the strong arms and the broad chest and that silly huge gun upon his hip. He has his own ghosts to deal with, and has grown as distant as the evening star. I can no longer speak with him."

"I'm sorry to hear that, Ophie."

"The only one I *can* talk to is Eddie."

"And what is the quality of his advice?"

"You might be surprised," I said. "Like you, he's fond of literature. But his tastes run more to Poe."

"A dark one, that bird."

"Takes after his mistress," I said.

We walked on, but this time in silence. We found the end of Chestnut Street, and walked it into town. The road was frozen hard beneath our feet. Our steps echoed in the still winter air like the rattle and scuffle of the dominoes pushed by old men in the lonely saloons.

We continued to the corner of First Avenue and North Front Street, then crossed to the northeast corner building with the big front window, with the fresh gold lettering that said

CALDER & WYLDE, CONSULTING DETECTIVES. This, imposed over a stylized Ace of Spades. Mitford, that jack-of-all-trades, had done a good job with the lettering, and none of the green paint on the frame had smudged any of the panes.

The interior of the agency was dark, as Calder was in the habit of spending his Sunday afternoons playing billiards at the Saratoga.

In the building just behind the agency, my neighbor, Mitford the undertaker, was at work. We could hear the bite and draw of a handsaw, and then the bark of a chisel, and I imagined wood chips clinging to Mitford's extravagant beard. In my mind, he was building a coffin, although he could have just as easily been working on an item meant for the living; most of his business was devoted to the selling of furniture. When Mitford wasn't building coffins or furniture, he was adding rooms to rent on the top floor of the establishment. A private staircase, protected from the elements by a roof, like a tiny covered bridge, descended from the second floor of the furniture shop to the detective agency. The stairs led from the back of the agency to my private bedroom above the furniture store, where a window overlooked my flat roof, Front Street beyond, and the Santa Fe tracks and depot.

I unlocked the door.

"Pardon me if I don't invite you to come in."

"I'm sure you have much writing to do," McCarty said, hands in his pockets. "The adventure waits to be distilled into thought. But if that work should prove insufficient to distract you from your cares, and if you believe that a bit of company would provide some relief—do not hesitate to call."

"Of course," I said.

I stepped inside the agency and softly closed the door behind me, then locked it. Eddie, who was perched on the plaster bust of Thomas Jefferson atop the high bookcase along the east wall, containing a complete set of Kansas statute books and assorted legal references, gave an impatient cry and stretched his wings.

"Hello, Eddie."

The raven swiveled his head to fix me with a questioning gaze.

"No oranges today," I said. "Tomorrow, perhaps, when the train comes. But none today."

Oranges, I thought. *If only my needs were as simple.*

I sat down at my desk, opened the bottom drawer, and stirred the contents. I would say I hadn't organized the drawer in a good spell, but the truth is, I had never done so; consequently, it was filled with bottles of ink and pens and clotted nibs and a handful of pencils, some broken, and many old newspapers I was keeping for reasons that were mysteries to me now. I was looking for something placed there not so long ago, however, something heavy that would have fallen to the bottom of the drawer. Finally, my fingers brushed something hard and smooth.

My hand emerged with an awkwardly shaped brass object mounted on a wooden base. It was a telegraph key, the kind that code practitioners refer to as a "camelback," because the long brass lever has a pronounced hump. Carefully, I placed the device on the desk. I gently touched a fingertip to the walnut button on the end of the lever, and the key began to chatter. As it clacked out a string of dits and dahs, a heatless blue flame danced over the instrument. But no electricity ran through it; it was connected to no wires, nor did it have a battery or other source of power.

When I removed my finger, the clicks and clacks continued. It was a peculiar sound, like a musical phrase, that repeated over and over.

I cannot understand Morse code, but the message was one that had been deciphered for me months before, and I had learned to recognize its rhythm. It was the only message that came from the key, and it repeated itself endlessly if the device wasn't stowed in some fashion to keep the lever depressed and immobile.

The message was from the book of Job 38: 35.

"Canst thou send lightnings, that they may go and say unto thee, 'Here we are?'"

I reached out and clamped my right hand over the key, silencing it. The blue flame leapt up, jittered for a moment across my knuckles, and then winked out.

Here we are, indeed. Mired on this side of life like poor Richard's horse in the mud, useless, and fatal to those who count upon you. How much wiser are the Werthers and the Chattertons, gladly sloughing off this world for the next.

I tucked the spirit telegraph back into the drawer, lever down, and slid the drawer closed. Then I placed my hands palms down on the desk and attempted to quiet the damned voice in my head.

You are twenty-nine years old. What chance now, for happiness?

"Shut up, shut up!" I shouted at myself, rising to my feet. "I can't stand the sound of you—of myself—any longer."

Consider your death.

"No," I said.

Give up the ghost.

A chill shook my frame.

I walked back to the stove, swung open the fire door with the poker, and tossed a few cotton-wood logs into the embers from the box beside the stove. Then I slammed the door and adjusted the damper, and watched through the mica glass as the fire bloomed.

Just close the damper.

"But that would kill Eddie, too."

Then I clapped my hands to my mouth, shocked that I was now negotiating with the voice in my head.

I found the pint bottle of whiskey Calder kept hidden on the shelf, behind a copy of Lew Wallace's *The Fair God,* a book he had never read but which he displayed as a prize because the territorial governor of New Mexico had given the book to him personally, as thanks for some kind of law enforcement work. There was also some Civil War history with Wallace that I did not understand, nor did I care to, because I had had my fill of the way men worshiped the memory of a mass slaughter of a generation. Glory was cheap when you were an old soldier recalling, from the comfort of an easy chair, the horrific events of thirteen years before.

The bottle had no label, but I remembered Calder called it "Taos Lightning." He said he kept it for emergencies, and I reckoned at that moment I myself was enough of an emergency. I had sworn off the hard stuff more than a year ago, shortly after I came to Dodge City and found myself adrift and soul-less; not only didn't I like the taste of whiskey, but I hated the mental dullness it induced.

At this moment, however, I needed some dullness.

I uncorked the bottle and took a long pull of the amber liquid. It smelled like varnish and tasted worse, and it burned its way down my throat to smolder in the pit of my stomach.

By the time I stoppered the bottle and returned it to the care of General Wallace, the contents were a third gone. I still hated the taste of the stuff, but at least the voice in the back of my head was, for the moment, silenced—even if the room did seem a bit off center now.

I went back to the desk, leaned against it, and took from my pocket the cube of paving stone McCarty had given me. I clasped it tightly in my hand as I stared out the window at the empty street, awash in hard winter sunlight.

The glass returned my reflection.

I stared back at myself, a slight figure dressed in black, save for a white shirt, and with a tangle of red hair falling to the shoulders. The face was just a shadow, as if I had already crossed over.

In days not long past, a familiar green face might appear in the glass, leering and telling bad jokes. But my ghostly companion from childhood had disappeared, perhaps for good, and only my reflection stared back from the depth of the glass, making me even more lonesome than before.

As I pondered my reflection, my thoughts ran to my life before Dodge City. What would have become of me had I continued the life of a confidence woman, a trance medium, a charlatan and a fraud? I had stolen fortunes, considerable and otherwise, from a string of men who were convinced of my otherworldly powers—and of my affection. To make others believe is the easiest thing in the world, and easier still if the thing presented is outrageous in desperate desire. The foolish frogs cannot help but pursue the golden ball.

The men I cheated, I told myself, were cheats themselves, and worse, and deserved the grim harvest of avarice and lust. I felt I was justified in this behavior. Thwarted by love at a tender age, robbed of happiness by death, corrupted by grief, and seduced by the dark side of prayer, I had a thousand reasons why the satisfied deserved to suffer.

None of that made it right, of course, and my reckless ways left many an unhappy heart behind.

My own unhappy heart I carried with me. Try as I might, I could never leave it behind, not in Chicago or St. Louis or Cincinnati. Then I fled west, and—as I have recounted before the tale—I was given a second chance, and began my life anew.

I thought I had finally left my heavy heart behind, but I had only placed the burden down for a moment. All of the old wounds still bled, along with a few fresh ones as well. As I stood looking at my image in the window, it seemed as if my heart would pull me down through the very floorboards of the agency to the dirt below.

The same earthly reward awaited both the righteous and the wicked.

I turned from the window and tossed the paving stone on the desk, where it skipped and spun across the walnut top as well as any die thrown in the Saratoga or the Long Branch. The stone came to rest just shy of the edge, its rough face revealing nothing of my future.

"We could return to the life," I suggested to Eddie. "It would be like the old days. Just me and you and a carpet bag of our necessary things and a copy of the blue book to tell us everything we need to know about the new town. And there is some thrill in being wicked."

Eddie craned his neck and stretched his wings, the tips of his feathers brushing down over the president's worried brow.

"So, what do you think, my friend?"

The raven mocked me with a raucous chuckle and flew with dash and determination from the top of Jefferson's head to his other favorite spot in the agency, the newel post at the bottom of the stairs that led up to the rented room above the furniture store.

"You're right, of course," I said. "You always are."

There was only one thing left to do.

I grasped the back of the chair and dragged it over to the bookcase containing the law books. Then I stepped up on the seat of the chair. The whiskey had made balance a matter to be negotiated, so I crouched like a cat for a few moments to get the hang of things, and then I cautiously stood fully upright.

I reached to the top shelf, still far above my head, and grasped the nearest of a series of books bound in leather and some sand-colored cloth. *Laws of Kansas, 1878*, the serious letters on the spine said.

Once I had the volume and myself safely down, I placed the book on the desk and thumbed impatiently through the pages of civil law. It didn't take long to find the statute on divorce—and the enumeration of grounds permitted in Kansas. These included bigamy, abandonment, adultery, habitual drunkenness, impotency, gross neglect of duty, extreme cruelty, fraudulent contract, conviction of a felony or imprisonment, and cases where the wife is pregnant by another man at the time of the marriage. The law also required a state residency of one year, that at least one of the marital parties live in the state, and that the case be filed in the county of residence.

I slammed the book closed.

It gave enough of a jar to the spirit telegraph in the desk drawer to elicit that familiar string of biblical dits and dahs. I opened the drawer and repositioned the key to jam the lever.

"Hush up," I told the device. "You got me into this mess. Now, be still while I get myself out of it."

Then felt I like some watcher of the skies
When a new planet swims into his ken;
Or like stout Cortez when with eagle eyes
He star'd at the Pacific—and all his men
Look'd at each other with a wild surmise—
Silent, upon a peak in Darien.

—John Keats, *On First Reading Chapman's Homer*

2

It was the fourteenth day of October, during that singular time of year when the heat of summer has passed and winter is still a holiday or so away, when the cottonwoods along the banks of the Arkansas River turn to gold, and when the harvest has filled both cellar and larder. I have always been more attuned to the fall than any other season, perhaps because of my naturally somber and melancholy nature, but if there has been any day in my life that you could point to and say that I was happy, this would be the day.

I had finished my labor for the second volume of psychical detection, and it was bundled safely in a hat box and on the eastbound Santa Fe train to make its eventual way to my editor, Mr. Garrick Sloane of Old Statehouse Publishers in Boston. A copy of the first volume was on my shelf, and I had subscribers across the country; nearly every day, the mail brought letters from people I had never heard of, but who had read my book, and were compelled to write because I had pleased

them, or angered them, or left them in some
state that they could not define, despite their
ability to form sentences. Some wrote asking for
help with their own mysteries and their own ghosts,
or asking for money, or proposing marriage.
The most creative letters were from those few
that warned of my impending eternal damnation;
the writers of these clearly delighted in describing the tortures that awaited me at the hands of
a merciful God.

A few of the letters I answered, if the writer was
courteous and able to spell *cat,* but most of them
had a kind of pathos that frightened me. The
amount of personal detail in these letters was
shocking—*I am hopelessly dependent on potassium
bromide and in my weakened state the ghost of my
dead father returns to humiliate me*—and revealed
clues that are more properly the domain of the
priest or the psychic, not a detective. But on this
day, my mind did not dwell on disturbed ram-
blings from strangers.

It was evening, not long after dusk, and the
sky was crushed velvet, pierced by the evening
star and smudged by a few clouds in the west. It
was unusually quiet, because at present there
were no cattle or trains or saloon music, and off
in the distance I could hear a lonesome coyote
calling to his brothers.

The air was so mild that the door to the agency
was propped open, using one of the unusually
heavy black stones the cowboys sometimes carry
in from the prairie; I allowed Eddie to come or go
as he pleased, having decided that it was criminal

to imprison such an intelligent animal in a cage, so the open doorway posed no special hazard. He seemed largely uninterested in the world beyond the doorway, however, and when he wasn't upstairs with me in the rented room, he spent most of his time monitoring the business of the agency from atop Lincoln's head.

I was sitting at my desk with a freshly brewed cup of tea, reading by lamplight the Kansas City and Topeka papers, making notes in a ledger about items I found of interest: the passenger steamer *Princess Alice* had sunk in the Thames after colliding with a collier, drowning 640 persons; the Edison Electric Light Company had, in New Jersey, unveiled a dynamo-powered system with which to illuminate entire city blocks, at a cost far below that of gas; and in Kansas, Dull Knife was still leading his followers toward the ancestral Cheyenne home on the northern plains, and raiding and killing along the way, despite the efforts of the U.S. Army and assorted local authorities to return them to the reservation in Indian Territory.

Then I put down my pen and rested my chin in my hand, pondering a dream I'd had the night before. The dream didn't frighten me, but it had been unusual, and it must have been that oddness that woke me—and what made me remember it later. I decided I should record the dream in the ledger book:

In my dream, I was standing in the middle of a large barn at night. The barn was dark and damp and had a sense of history about it; the upper wooden part

*rested on a stone foundation that was warped with age.
Behind me, the double doors were open.*

*The night was clear and a nearly full moon was just
above the trees. Enough moonlight came in through the
doorway that I could see my shadow on the straw and
dirt floor in front of me. It was cold in the barn, because I could see my breath, but I wasn't cold; I had on
several layers of clothes, so much so that it was difficult
to bend my arms and legs.*

*From somewhere in the back of the barn, in the dark-
est part, came the raspy call of a barn owl.*

"Don't," I said.

But the owl kept calling.

*I stepped forward, peering into the cavernous barn,
but could make nothing out. It did not seem to me that
Eddie was near, because otherwise I would have been
worried for his safety; also, I seemed quite alone, far removed from the possibility of any human company, but
the impression, rather than a cause for concern, was
oddly familiar and comforting.*

"It's too dark," I said, and turned back.

*Then the rasp of the barn owl came again, more in-
sistently.*

*With difficulty, I reached into one of my many pock-
ets and emerged with a lit taper (as such things are
possible in dreams). Far at the end of the candle's circle
of light I saw the shining white face of the barn owl, as
if daring me to approach.*

*I stepped forward, and saw the owl was atop a nest,
tucked between the stone foundation and the wooden
side of the barn. The nest was about the size of a hatbox
and contained many small branches and a few shavings
and splinters. As I approached, the owl turned its*

*heart-shaped face, and the candle flame was twinned
in its large dark eyes.*

"What now?"

*The owl was silent, but it was somehow clear to me
that I was to reach down inside the nest. As I stretched
my arm out, I found that my reach was no longer
encumbered by clothes; not only was my arm bare, but
so was my entire body. I was now cold and began to
shiver, and was afraid of what might be in the owl nest,
but I climbed up on the stone foundation and forced
myself to reach down into the nest. My fingertips
touched hard, old brittle things that I knew were the
bones of small animals, and some fresh moist things
that were too disgusting to even think about. Then my
fingers touched some hard and tube-shaped thing, and
I grasped it and brought it out. It was a small brass
cylinder, green with age, attached by a band to a skele-
tal bird's leg.*

*I removed the tube's knurled cap, and discovered a
tightly wound piece of paper inside. It was obvious the
coiled paper was a message of some intent, perhaps
secret, certainly lost in transmission.*

At that moment I glimpsed from the corner
of my eye a streak of light on the southern hori-
zon. I looked up, thinking it was an odd time for
a storm, and scanned the sky, but saw nothing
that resembled lightning. After a moment, I returned to my ledger book.

*I knew the message was important, and meant for
me, but I had no clue about who might have sent it.
How odd, I thought, that there were no spectral messen-
gers here. I heard no voices, saw no apparitions, but*

*was confronted instead with a very practical method of
communicating over long distances.*

*I tried tapping the slip of paper out on my other palm
(somehow the candle had vanished, but still could I
see), but the paper wouldn't come. But before I could
tease out the paper—with its presumed message—the
barn shook and*

I stopped scribbling, because I heard some
commotion from the depot, a half a block to the
south. I looked up in time to see Mackie, the station's telegrapher, standing in the middle of
Front Street, imploring Wyatt Earp to help him.
From the way Earp stood, with his arms folded
across his chest, he appeared unmoved by the
appeal. But Mackie, a small birdlike man with a
wisp of gray hair on the top of his head, was in-
sistent; he clutched the sleeve of Earp's shirt and
attempted to drag him toward the depot.

"What's the trouble?" Doc McCarty asked from
the doorway. "I heard Mackie all the way down
at my place. Is it a health crisis?"

"I don't know."

"Then we'd better find out," McCarty said.

I took another quick sip of my tea, then followed.

Earp remained with his arms folded, with the
little man circling around him. Earp was the assistant city marshal, and had been on and off the
local police force several times in the last two
years, once having gone to Deadwood in the
Dakotas in pursuit of fortune and then spending some weeks pursuing unspecified affairs in
Texas. I had met Earp while investigating a case

back in the summer, and had formed a not very favorable impression of the thirty-year-old marshal. Nothing had happened since then to convince me otherwise.

Mackie took hold of Earp's sleeve and tried to tug him toward the depot, but the marshal jerked his arm away.

"Stop it, or I will give you the what for," Earp warned, it seemed, a bit louder and more threatening than the situation allowed. "Do not drag me over there to look at your nonsense."

Mackie was talking so fast that I could only catch part of what he was saying, but I did hear the word *fire* repeated.

"What's on fire?" McCarty asked.

"*Blue* fire," Mackie said. "Shooting out of the key to dance across my fingers. Nonsense coming from the sounder, and the wire all tied up. Please, I'm afraid to go back into the station by myself."

"Sounds like Mackie has been drinking," Earp said.

"Of course I've been drinking," the telegrapher said. "There isn't much else to do on a lonely night like this. But I'm not drunk, and I know what I saw and heard, and you'd believe me if you would just—"

At that moment, a falling star streaked across the sky, like the most brilliant fireworks display you'd ever seen, except brighter and grander. The star was sparkling white, with hints of red and green, and it broke into a shower of golden sparks somewhere above the southern plains.

"Did you see that?" Mackie asked.

"Hard to miss," Earp said.

Two more stars fell, spectacularly.

"That's odd," McCarty said.

Now, while one celestial event may inspire a warm and hopeful feeling, three introduce something between confusion and dread. Smaller fireballs were now zinging overhead, tipping the scale decidedly toward dread.

"It's the end of the world," Mackie said.

"I've heard no trumpets," Earp said. I could not tell whether he was making a joke or was being serious, and before I could make up my mind there was another considerable pyrotechnic display to admire.

"It's a meteor shower," McCarty said. "A spectacular one, but only a meteor shower. It is not the end of anything."

Then we saw something that resembled a shimmering curtain of pink and green undulate across the sky. The wires hanging between the telegraph poles began to glow blue, faintly at first, and then brighter. Sparks dripped from the wires, scattering on the ground or sliding down the roof of the depot.

"Will it burn?" Mackie asked.

"Yes, Doc," I said. "Is this sort of thing to be expected from a meteor shower?"

"No."

"Is it likely going to set anything on fire?" I asked.

"I don't know," McCarty said. "I've never read about anything similar, except perhaps Saint

Elmo's fire on the tops of the masts of ships at sea. But that's associated with electrical storms, not meteor showers."

"Whatever it is," Earp said, "I don't like it."

"I tried to tell you something was wrong," Mackie said. "The telegraph was going crazy. Ghosts are on the line."

"Show us," McCarty said.

"Not me," Earp said.

"Come now," McCarty said. "You have a reputation for being fearless. You're not afraid, are you, Wyatt?"

"I just don't have time for this," Earp growled.

"Leave him," I said. "Mackie, show me the trouble."

With the lines overhead still sparking, we dashed down the street to the depot and climbed the steps to the platform. Earp hesitated, and then ran after us. Even from outside the station, we could hear the clatter coming from inside, a barrage of dits and dahs punctuated by the occasional electric crackle and pop.

Mackie led us past the ticket windows into the station master's office, the walls of which were covered with drawers and cubbyholes and where an octagonal-faced clock marked time with a lazy brass pendulum. On the mainline track side of the depot was a bay window, and beneath the windows a desk with assorted telegraph apparatus connected to wires going to the outside. I can't tell you what all of the equipment was, but I did recognize the telegraph key and the sounding box. The jittering key was wreathed in blue flame, and ghostly smoke was rising from the sounder, which was chattering so hard that I feared its cabinet would crack.

"What's it saying?" Calder asked.

"Which one?" Mackie said. "The key is sending, but there are four or five other fists coming through the sounder. The first message I heard is the one the key is sending now. 'Canst thou send lightnings, that they may go, and say unto thee, Here we are?' It's not unusual for an operator in the pay of one of the wire services to keep the line open by sending Bible verses, but this one just keeps repeating. It's a fist I don't recognize."

"What do you mean, 'fist'?" McCarty asked.

"All operators develop a distinctive style of sending, which is called their fist. We call it this because you use your whole hand to send, in a motion that comes from the wrist, and involves more than just your fingers on the lever. Once you get the hang of it, recognizing an operator by his fist is as easy as recognizing one of your friends from the sound of his voice. I know all of the operators on the circuit, and whoever is sending the Bible passage has a fist that is strange to me."

"Can you determine his location from what you hear?" McCarty asked.

"That's the thing," Mackie said. "The key is *sending*, it's not receiving. The message is originating from here, at that desk, yet there is no finger visible upon the key."

"So, it's haunted," Earp said. His face was unusually pale.

"Let's not jump to conclusions," McCarty said. "There may be some reasonable explanation that we've overlooked. What we need is to make a list, and think of all the possible causes for the key to act in such a manner, and systemically check them off the list. Ah, there's a pad of paper and a pencil over there on the counter. Would you mind handing it to me, Mr. Mackie?"

"There's a simpler way to check this out," Earp said.

"Oh?" McCarty asked.

Earp drew a heavy knife and placed the blade down on the insulated wires at the back of the telegraph key. Then he made a fist with his other hand and brought it down sharply on the knife, severing the leads. The blue flame entered the knife and swirled up Earp's wrist. He jumped back as if he had been bitten by a rattlesnake, and shook his hand so violently the knife flew out and clattered on the floor.

But the unearthly flame flared and vanished.

"Did it hurt?" I asked.

"No," he said, retrieving his knife. "It surprised me. Felt prickly is all."

The key was silent now.

"May I?" I asked, reaching my hand toward the key.

"Go ahead," Mackie said.

I picked up the instrument, which was surprisingly heavy. I looked at the hump-shaped lever, and the flat button on the end, and the spring beneath and the adjustment screws. On the side of the lever, neatly stamped into the brass, was the legend: "AVAIL SPEEDWELL."

The key continued to tap out its message.

"It's detached," Earp said. "Should it still be doing that?"

"It's completely removed from the circuits," Mackie said, fear making his voice tremble. "It shouldn't be doing anything, much less sending at thirty words a minute. Please, Miss Wylde, could you take the key with you when you go? I don't want it here in the office with me."

"Don't blame you," Earp said.

The other messages were still rocking the sounder.

Then the wireless key stopped for several seconds, and then began again, but with a different message, at a slower pace.

"Wait," Mackie said. "That's one fist I recognize."

He picked up the pad and pencil and began to copy.

"Who is it?" I asked.

"Hopkins," he said, continuing to copy the message even as he talked. "He was the operator at Florence, in Marion County, about four hours down the tracks to the east. But it can't be."

When Mackie stopped writing, he had a queer look on his face.

"What's it say?" Earp asked.

Mackie handed over the pad, and I leaned close to Earp's shoulder to read the message:

I AM MURDERED!

3

"Murdered," Earp said, regarding the telegraph key with suspicion. "He's being murdered and has the time to send a message?"

"No," Mackie said. "Hopkins—or Hapless Hopkins, as everyone called him, because he was the unluckiest operator to ever touch a key—collapsed and died a week ago this Sunday, after eating his dinner. It was assumed his heart failed him."

"Hopkins seems to think otherwise," I said.

"Were you and this Hopkins friends?" Earp asked.

"Yes," he said. "The key is his, in fact; it was his personal key, the one he was using the night he died, and his friends thought he would have wanted me to have it. It is old, and quite a fine key, although I've never seen another one exactly like it. The name of the manufacturer is stamped in the brass, SPEEDWELL, but it is a concern I've never heard of."

"A mystery," McCarty said, smiling.

"When is the next train to Florence?" I asked.

"The eastbound combination, the *Ginery Twitchell*," Mackie said.

"I'd like to be on it," I said.

"Don't be silly," Earp said. "You don't even have a client."

"Whenever there's a murder accompanied by messages from the grave, I'm guessing I can find a client."

"You might not be going anywhere anytime soon," Mackie said. "With all this nonsense on the circuit, I don't know if it's on time or hopelessly delayed. I have no way to receive updates from the dispatcher, or to send reports of my own. This intelligence is necessary to put a train on a siding to allow another to pass; otherwise, collisions are assured on a single-track railway."

"What's the chance this phenomenon is only manifesting at this depot?" McCarty asked.

"The circuit is common," Mackie said. "If it's happening here, it's happening everywhere, and if it lasts for more than a few minutes, it will bring the Santa Fe to its knees. The timetable is king. The railway runs on the clock and the telegraph; without the latter, the entire line is in confusion, and lives are in jeopardy."

"Perhaps things will settle before the train arrives," McCarty said.

"And if they don't?" Earp asked.

Mackie pursed his lips.

The *Ginery Twitchell* was scheduled to arrive at seven, he said, and then wait on a siding for the westbound freight to pass ten minutes later. It wouldn't take much of a deviation from the schedule on the part of either train for things to end in disaster.

"Is there any way to stop them?"

"I can lower the ball," he said, referring to the bright red ball on the mast outside. "Low ball means stop at the station, but it's night and the westbound freight will be expecting to highball it through and may not be able to stop in time, if it meets the combination."

"Then we'll have to flag them down well before they near the station," McCarty said. "Mackie, you stay here in case the lines clear. The rest of us will flag down the trains."

Mackie broke out a pair of railway lanterns, checked that each had oil, and lit them. He gave one lantern to McCarty and offered the other to Earp, who hesitated.

"There is business I must attend to."

"Oh, for God's sake," I said, and took the lantern. The globe was oddly shaped, like an elongated pumpkin, but clear red, and encased in a kind of bird cage affair to protect the glass.

"You go west, Ophelia," McCarty said, already on his way out the door. "I'll head east."

"What do I do with it?" I asked.

"Just swing it in front of you," Mackie said. "The engineer will see it."

I left the station, hurried down the platform, and set off down the railway tracks in the direction of Colorado. The lantern threw enough light from the bottom to allow me to see where I was stepping, but I still had to be careful, because the spaces between the ties were full of loose stones, cinders, and the occasional plate or spike. But soon I fell into a rhythm of stepping from one tie to the next, and followed the tracks into the dark and seemingly endless prairie. The wire stretched over the telegraph poles was still glowing and giving off an occasional shower of sparks, but not as energetically as before.

The eastbound must have been late, because I know I'd walked for more than ten minutes without seeing anything at the end of the track.

It felt more than a bit odd to be alone at night carrying a red lantern down the center of a pair of railway tracks, and I briefly pondered whether there might be any wolves or panthers or two-legged killers watching my passage, from among the shadows in the tall grass. The thought made me feel slightly silly—could I really be frightened so easily?—but then I heard footsteps on the roadbed behind me.

My heart skipped three beats.

"Ophelia."

It was Earp.

"Stop for a moment," he said.

I had to catch my breath before I could speak.

"Were you trying to frighten me on purpose?" I asked.

"Why would I do that?"

"Only you would know," I said.

"Well, I wasn't trying to scare you," he said. "I was coming after to say you'd gone far enough. If it were daylight, you'd see that we're at the top of a low hill, and there's a clear line of sight down the tracks for a couple of miles."

"I thought you had some errand to run," I said.

"I said I had something to attend to," he said. "It took only a moment."

I placed the lantern down on a tie between us. It bathed our legs in a strange red glow.

"What could be so important when catastrophe is in the air?"

"A friend was in desperate need," he said.

"The dentist?" I asked.

Not long after Earp had returned from Texas, a sometime dentist and full-time gambler and consumptive named Doc Holliday arrived in Dodge. He and Earp had met at Fort Griffin and had apparently been fast friends from the start.

"Yes, Holliday. He has suffered rather badly today, and I was bringing him a box of Dr. Pierce's Pleasant Pellets to provide some relief. It took only a moment to deliver the box, and only two people were needed to propel the lanterns."

"The prime ingredient in Dr. Pierce's pellets is the poppy," I said. "You are doing your friend no favors."

"You have not witnessed his suffering."

"I did not think opium was an anodyne typically prescribed for consumption."

"He has other ills," Earp said, wounded at my lack of sympathy for his new friend.

"Don't we all," I said.

"Look," Earp said, nodding down the track.

A pinpoint of light had appeared.

"Better get to signaling," Earp said. "At their speed, they will be upon us in three or four minutes."

I picked up the lantern and began to move it, at waist level, stiffly from side to side.

"No," Earp said, stepping close to me. "You've got to swing it."

He closed his hands over mine and pushed the lantern down to my knees. I could feel his chest pressing against my back, but before I could decide if it was a pleasant feeling or not, he was giving me instructions. "Now, let it swing natural, like a pendulum, and slow. Yes, that's it."

The lamp made a wide and low red arc.

"Why do you avoid me?" he asked.

His breath was coffee and cigar smoke.

"This is hardly the time," I said.

"Your disapproval is obvious."

"I hardly know you," I said. "Besides, it is you who has no affection for me."

"You are mistaken," he said. "I am strangely attracted."

"It was never my ambition to be a strange attractor."

"By strangely, I meant—"

I decided the closeness was unpleasant.

"Marshal Earp," I said, breaking away. "You are married."

Well, that was overstating the case somewhat. He had a common-law wife named Mattie whom he had met in a brothel back in Wichita, as I understood it, and she had continued her career. It was not an unusual arrangement on the frontier, but one that I found distasteful. In my former life, it wouldn't have caused me a second's thought, but since assuming my new straight life, I had gotten downright puritanical about such things.

"It is a temporary arrangement," he said.

"Perhaps, but you are nonetheless occupied," I said. "Please, let us attend to the business at hand. We can parse our grotesque affections later."

The light down the track had grown closer and we could hear the chugging sound of the engine, and feel the vibration transmitted by the rails to the track bed. I kept lazily swinging the lamp, hoping the engineer was alert and watching the track ahead and would not run over me and slice me into a thousand strips of uncanny jerky.

"It doesn't seem to be slowing," I said.

"It takes them a long time to stop," Earp said. "If you listen carefully, you can hear the beat of the rods slowing. There, now we can hear the protests of the jostling cars as the air brakes are applied."

"Yes, I hear it now."

I kept swinging the lantern.

The train's progress became a crawl. When it was within a hundred yards, I was illuminated by the headlight, and could feel the size and immensity of the locomotive behind it.

The *Ginery Twitchell* was a beast, with two drive wheels taller than I was on each side, and a cab behind the boiler that seemed like a small house. The engineer was leaning far out from the lofty window of the cab, trying to see as much ahead of him as possible, uncertain as to why he was being flagged down.

Earp grasped my arm and pulled me off the tracks as the *Ginery Twitchell* came to a tortured metallic halt a few yards from us, then hissed and belched steam.

"What's the trouble?" the engineer called.

"The telegraph is down," Earp said, taking hold of a grab iron and pulling himself up the steps that led to the cab.

"Hell, that ain't nothing," the engineer said, and spat tobacco juice to the ground twelve feet below. "The telegraph is always down somewhere. The crudding Cheyenne cut the wires two or three weeks ago about twenty miles west and it took—"

Earp drew his revolver and fired a round into the air.

"You make me want to punch you in the throat," he said. "Shut up and listen. The entire railway telegraph network, from Topeka to New Mexico, may be inoperable. The station agent sent us out to flag you down and keep you from colliding with the westbound freight."

The engineer pulled a twist of tobacco from his pocket and sliced off a bit with his pocket knife. His eyes, however, were fixed on the gun in Earp's hand.

"Don't come any closer to the cab," he said.

"Why?"

"Because your story stinks like a wet dog," the engineer said, slipping the chunk of tobacco into his mouth. "And because I've got a ten-gauge shotgun here in the cab and I'm not shy about using it. Holster that sidearm and let us pass."

"You believe we're here to rob you?"

"Somebody flagging down a train at night is never up to any good."

"My name's Wyatt Earp and I'm a Dodge City marshal."

"Never heard of you."

The engineer pushed a lever and the train lurched forward, shaking the slack out of the line of cars behind. A series of metal thunderclaps shook the prairie.

Earp swore.

"Holster that weapon," I said.

As the locomotive's huge drive wheels began to roll, I approached the cab with my hands visible, both hands on the bale of the lantern.

"Please," I shouted. "You must stop."

"Who are you?"

"A friend," I said.

"You could be a member of the James Gang, for all I know."

"I'm Ophelia Wylde and I'm a resident of Dodge City and a tax-paying business owner and I know the man at the depot at Dodge is named Mackie and that his friend, Hopkins, of the fraternity of railway telegraphers, died unexpectedly in Marion County."

"Step back," the engineer growled.

"Fils de salope," I swore. *Sonuvabitch.*

I kicked the ground, scattering rocks toward the hulking locomotive and its pigheaded engineer. Anger clouded my brain so that I could no longer form a coherent sentence in English, but I had no trouble issuing a melodious string of French Creole curses.

Then a voice rang in the center of my mind, hard and clear and right.

"Winnie tells you to stop," I shouted.

The engineer jammed another lever forward and the locomotive lost its momentum.

"What did you say?"

"Winnifred says to stop," she said. "She's telling me that if you don't, you're not only going to kill yourself, but your fireman will die too, and some of your passengers. Winnie tells me to remind you of what happened in Plymouth."

The engineer applied the air brakes and the train came to a complete stop.

"What do you know of Plymouth?"

"Nothing," I said. "But Winnie does."

"I was nearly killed at Plymouth, in Lyon County, when a fool pulled a pin on a freight car and it nearly crushed me against a track bumper. It was during a thunderstorm, it was raining snakes and frogs, and I didn't hear the car rolling toward me—but I heard Winnie's voice telling me to get out of the way."

In the glare from the firebox, I could see the lines in the engineer's face, the deep-set and sad eyes, the mustache stained with tobacco juice.

"Winnie was my little sister," he said. "She's been dead twenty years. Typhoid. And I've never told anyone the story about what happened during the thunderstorm at Plymouth. So how do you know it?"

"All I can tell you is that I heard her voice."

"Can you still hear her?"

"No," I said. "She's gone."

The engineer nodded.

"You're that psychical detective and professor of mediumship, who speaks to the dead, that I've read about in the newspapers, aren't you?"

I said I was.

"Climb up, Professor," he said. "There's a siding a mile back, built back in seventy-two when this was the end of track, and it's long enough to get all of our cars off the main line."

4

I handed the lantern to Earp, then took the first couple of iron steps up to the cab. Earp started to climb up after me, but the engineer spat.

"Not him," he said.

"Why not?"

"Just not."

"He's right," I said.

"You don't like me, either?"

"No, I mean you have to go back and tell Mackie the *Ginery Twitchell* is safely sided," I said. "I'll stay with the train until Mackie sends word that the main line is clear and we can proceed safely."

"All right," Earp said. "I have things to do in town, anyway."

Earp jumped down and made a show of brushing dust from his clothes, then started walking back toward Dodge, swinging the lantern lazily beside him. As the engineer put the train in reverse, and we backed away, slowly at first, and then faster, I watched as the lantern grew ever smaller.

"Thank you for stopping," I said. The cab was rocking and I braced against the wall.

"I should have stopped sooner," the engineer said. He was looking intently out the side window at the track behind us or, rather, ahead of us.

"No, your suspicion was understandable."

"My suspicion may have killed us all," he said, easing the throttle open. The train increased its speed to what seemed to me an alarming rate.

"What's wrong?" I asked.

"There's a train behind us," he said. "Three or four miles behind us, but if it's highballing, and you add our combined speeds, that means we're coming together at seventy miles an hour. That gives us less than four minutes to tuck ourselves away on the siding."

"What train is it?"

"Damned if I know," he said. "There were no orders for another until midnight."

He grabbed a cord overhead and gave a series of short blasts on the train's whistle. The shriek was alarmingly loud in the cab, and added to the cacophony of the chugging locomotive and cars rattling on the tracks.

"Don't know if he can see me or hear me," he said. "If he's traveling at any speed, he might be upon us before he spots the red lamps on the caboose. It's clear, though, so he should. But I hate betting our lives on should."

He eased off the throttle now, and we began to slow.

"Garrity," the engineer called to the stoker, who was gathering up chunks of wood from the tender and throwing them into the firebox. "Throw down that timber and make your way back in a hurry. Find the brakeman. As soon as we've slowed enough, jump down and run back to the switch. If I'm remembering this section of track right, the caboose should be within fifty or a hundred yards of the switch. Take a bar and a sledge-hammer with you. The switch may be a bit rusty, and there will likely be a padlock on it, which you'll have to break. Tell me you understand."

"Aye," the brakeman said. "I'm to move my arse right quick."

"Go then," the engineer said.

He disappeared over the top of the tender.

I moved to the other side of the cab so I'd have a clear view behind us. The yellow head-light of the other train flared and wobbled in the darkness.

"It doesn't appear to be slowing," I said.

"It's not," said the engineer. Then he applied the air brakes and the train screeched and shuddered as we came to a stop. "Jump clear while you have time," he urged.

"And risk being taken for a coward?" I asked. "Thanks, but I'll play this hand."

The engineer grunted and peered behind us. We could see the lamps of Garrity and the brakeman, hear the sound of the sledge striking metal, and their cursing.

"Get on with it," the engineer said, then spat out the window.

The sledge struck three more blows, then there was a pause, and a final blow and a clank. A moment later, we could hear the sound of the rusty switch being turned.

"Good, boys," the engineer said. "That's it."

Then they signaled with the lantern to proceed.

I looked back and saw the headlight of the other train clearly now. Instead of just a spot of light, I could see a cold blue flame and its sheen on the cowcatcher and the rails beneath.

"They're not stopping," I said. "In fact, it looks like they're picking up speed."

The engineer cursed as he released the brakes, hurriedly spun some valves, and then he opened the throttle. I could hear the hiss of live steam rush to the cylinders, and then the drivers engaged the wheels, which spun for a moment before finding purchase. The train jumped, and somewhere in the line of cars behind us I heard the metallic ping of metal shearing.

"Dammit," the engineer said.

"What's wrong?" I asked.

"I've broken a pin," he said.

"Is that bad?"

"The pins keep the cars coupled," he said. "I don't know where, but somewhere I've broken us in two. We use straight air, so their brakes won't work."

As the end of the train was pushed and snaked onto the siding, I had a clearer view of the approaching train, which seemed like some black behemoth from beyond, all silent and promising catastrophe.

The mystery train passed our caboose—which was rolling free on the siding, along with two other cars, behind where the pin had broken—and was now within an eighth of a mile of us. But the locomotive and a half-dozen cars were still on the main line.

The engineer gave a little more throttle.

We were now in the cone of the black train's headlamp, and I realized that if we collided, my side of the cab would be approximately the point of impact. My heart felt like it would burst and I gripped the side of the cab tightly to keep from dropping to my knees. There was no use jumping at this point; if I did, I'd only be jumping onto the tracks in front of the onrushing locomotive.

So I did the only thing I could do.

I closed my eyes.

"Turn the switch, boys!" I heard the engineer shout. "Turn it now!"

The hot wind from the passing locomotive brushed my face, and the roar and clatter were fearsome. The train had not slowed at all, but was inexplicably continuing at top speed, and as it passed, our engineer leaned on the air whistle, and gave out a long shriek of protest.

I opened my eyes and watched the black train disappear down the main line. There were only three cars behind the locomotive and tender, an express car and two passenger cars, and no caboose. They were all painted in a dark color, perhaps black, and there appeared to be no numbers or letters on any of the cars.

Then there was a grinding sound behind us, and we watched as our slowly rolling caboose and its two cars met the bumper at the end of the siding. The caboose crashed through the heavy timbers and its wheels sank into the prairie soil, while the next car jammed itself into the vestibule of the caboose and splintered the roof.

Then the caboose came to a stop, rocking slightly.

"Come on, boys," the engineer said. "Let me see all of you."

The crew jumped out and waved.

The engineer gave a couple of blasts on the whistle in acknowledgment.

Then he spat out the window, crossed his arms, and looked down the tracks to the east, where the mystery train had disappeared into the darkness.

"Well done," I said.

"I broke a pin."

"But we are all in one piece," I said. "It was a narrow escape, and for a moment I thought it was certain catastrophe, but you saved us. And brother, I don't even know your name."

"Skeen," he said. "Alistair Skeen."

"Bravo, Engine Driver Skeen."

"Don't be too thankful," he said. "We may have just passed trouble down to the next section."

Then I thought about McCarty and was worried for him.

"Did you recognize that train?"

"That is the most troubling part," Skeen said.

"Why?"

"It wasn't one of ours," he said. "Not only were the colors all wrong, but we don't have a configuration like that. The train did not belong on the Santa Fe tracks."

Skeen began working the maze of valves and levers in front of him, bringing the steam pressure down to a safe level. Then there was a commotion on the ground below the cab, and I peered down to see a nattily dressed boy of about twenty with a lantern calling up to us.

"You there, in the cab."

"What is it?" Skeen grumbled.

"Not you, Mr. Skeen," the young man said. "The other gentleman, the one that flagged us down."

I leaned out of Skeen's window.

"I'm no gentleman," I said, "but will I do?"

"Begging your pardon," the young man said. "I had assumed, well, that you were a man. Garrity, the fireman, told us the story, but obviously he omitted some details."

"Obviously," I said.

The young man was wearing nankeen trousers, fashionably rumpled, and a thistle print cotton vest over a blue linen shirt. He had a head of unruly hair that was the same wheat color as his pants.

"In any case, miss, the general manager would like a word."

"The general manager?" I asked, now suspicious. "That wouldn't be anything like a superintendent, would it?"

"Well, I'm not sure."

"Is this general manager a human being?"

"What an odd question."

"Not for me."

"I can assure you that William Barstow Strong is not only a human being, but a fine individual from a respected Vermont family. Since assuming his duties in 1873, he has been made general manager *and* vice president in recognition of his efforts to extend the reach of the Santa Fe deep into Colorado, and even now is on his return journey from taking a personal survey of the technical problem posed by Raton Pass, which is our only barrier to New Mexico Territory."

"Sounds like a regular Cornelius Vanderbilt."

"Oh, no," the young man said. "I'm afraid Mr. Strong is a very down-to-earth sort, and would never have any truck with Spiritualists or ladies of questionable virtue."

"I should think not," I said. "What's your name?"

"Delmar Delaney," he said. "I'm Mr. Strong's personal secretary—some would say his confidante, even—and you can trust me to treat your personal affairs with the same discretion as the general manager's."

"I'll make up my own mind about whom to trust."

"Please, if you'll follow me," the young man said. "The general manager is most anxious to speak with you."

"I would like Mr. Skeen to come with me."

"Why?"

"Him, I trust."

"Go ahead, Professor," Skeen said. "The general manager won't allow me near him, because I'm a member of the Brotherhood of Railway Engineers. In April, the brotherhood shut down Emporia Junction and Topeka in protest of reduced wages and longer hours. The strike lasted four days before the governor, who is in the pocket of the railroad, called in federal troops."

Skeen spat tobacco juice over the side, and the missile came dangerously close to discoloring Delaney's pant cuff.

"Besides, I must stay with the engine," Skeen said. "The beast won't tend itself. But if you get in trouble, Professor, you just give the signal."

"What signal?"

"You whistle, of course."

I descended the steps and hopped down, refusing the hand that Delaney, the brash young man of the wheat-colored hair and enormous head, offered. We walked past the express car, then past a number of passenger cars, where the inhabitants were now spilling out, and then to a private car. Like all the rest of the cars, including the boxcars that followed it, the private car was predominantly yellow—the official Santa Fe color.

Beside the car, one man in a dark vest and rolled-up shirtsleeves was readying a spool of wire while another, in denim work clothes, was already halfway up a telegraph pole, a pair of wire spring clips in one hand. They both were my age, or a bit younger. The sky above was clear and filled with constellations, but no falling stars. To the north, however, the odd red and green ribbons of lights still danced.

We stepped up to the vestibule of the car, and Delaney held the door open as I stepped inside.

The interior of the car was brilliantly lit, and solidly—if not richly—appointed. There were a few padded chairs, but most of the car was filled with worktables bearing route maps and blueprints of bridges and other railway business. There was a telegraph key and sounder at one of the desks, and behind it in a straight-backed chair was a man of about forty years of age, with a high forehead, dark hair slicked back, and a graying beard that reached down to his stomach.

"Yes?" the bearded man asked, impatiently.

"Mr. Strong," the young man said. "May I present—"

"Miss Wylde," I said. "Ophelia Wylde."

"There was some confusion on the part of Garrity the fireman," the young man said. "But it was Miss Wylde who was involved in flagging us down."

"A woman," Strong said.

"Since birth," I said.

I held out my hand, and he took it cautiously. He pressed it, in that odd way some men have, but did not shake it.

"Would you like a cup of tea?" Delaney asked. Thinking of the tea I had abandoned earlier, I accepted. The young man disappeared toward the rear of the car.

"Forgive me if I dispense with the usual courtesies," Strong said. "Pull up a chair, please, and tell me why you felt compelled to stop the *Ginery Twitchell*."

As concisely as I could, I related the events of the night, beginning with Mackie asking for help in the middle of the street. But I omitted the part about how I had convinced Skeen to yield.

"That is all very curious," Strong said.

"It was more than curious," I said. "It was otherworldly, uncanny, and downright weird."

"Yes, I imagine it would seem that way."

"Of course it was that way," I said.

The men who had attached the jumpers to the telegraph line came inside the car.

"Pardon me a moment," Strong said to me. Then he turned to his pair of employees. "Are we tapped in, gentlemen?"

The man in the denim said the connection had been made.

"Then let us close the circuit," Strong said, and moved a blade on the base of the telegraph key. A puff of blue smoke emanated from the apparatus, and the sounder began to chatter, much like the one at the Dodge City depot had.

"How odd," the man in denim said. "So many messages at once."

"I believe I can pick something out," the man in the vest and shirtsleeves said, and sat down at the table and began to copy the code with a pencil. He wrote out a few more lines, but then frowned.

"This can't be."

"And yet," Strong said. "Tell me."

"It's a message to John Pemberton, the Confederate general in command of Vicksburg during the siege," he said. "It says, 'Expect no help from this side of the river.'"

"Ridiculous," Strong said.

"There's another message, a Bible verse—"

"The one about lightnings and 'here we are'?" I asked.

"The very one."

"Nonsense, Lawson," Strong said. "It is just noise on the wires."

The key began furiously tapping, amid a great ball of blue sparks. Smoke began to curl up.

"It might ruin the batteries," Lawson said.

"It's about to set the desk on fire," the man in denim said.

"Disconnect it, Mr. Salisbury," the general manager said.

The man in denim, Salisbury, unscrewed the wires, and burned his thumb in the process. He put the smarting digit to his lips. The cacophony of tapping and chattering slowly died away.

Both Lawson and Salisbury expressed relief.

Then, improbably, just as it had back in Dodge,

the sounder began to vibrate and the key to click again. This time, however, the racket was louder.

"There is no rational explanation for it," Lawson declared.

"It might be the end of the world," Salisbury said.

"That's what Mackie thought," I said. "But we're still here."

Strong looked out the window at the odd lights in the northern sky.

"Of course, there *is* an explanation," he said. "There always is. The natural world jealously guards her secrets, but surrender them, she must, eventually, to men of reason and steady disposition."

I wanted to punch him in the throat.

"What explanation could there be?" Lawson asked.

"None of you are old enough to remember this, but in late August and early September of 1859 the entire telegraphic systems *of the world* were paralyzed because of a peculiar atmospheric condition," Strong said. "The wires became hot, cells exploded, some devices did burst into flame. For three days, there was just noise on the line, and it was nigh to impossible to send a message. Batteries were disconnected, and yet current still flowed through the circuits. In truth, the lines were somewhat more usable when the cells were switched off. And there were lights in the sky, just as we see now."

"But how?" Salisbury asked.

"It is the northern lights we're seeing, rare for

this latitude, but not unheard of," Strong said. "In 1859, they were seen as far south as the Indian Ocean. In the Rocky Mountains, miners got up and went to work at midnight, believing dawn had come. In San Francisco, the lights were bright enough to read the smallest newsprint. And in New Orleans, crowds gathered in Jackson Square to alternately admire and fear the celestial display."

"I remember the lights," I said. "I was eleven years old, and we lived near Memphis. My Tante Marie led me out in the fields to see the sky. But these lights seem different. There were no falling stars back then."

What I didn't say is that Tante Marie had knelt beside me in the field and whispered in my ear that the mantle of fire in the sky was a sign that God's judgment would wash the stain of chattel slavery from the land.

"What caused them?" the man with the pencil asked.

"The theories were various," Strong said. "Some believed that volcanic debris from a Pacific island eruption was responsible, others concluded that the display was the result of sunlight reflecting from icebergs in the far north, and some felt that it was caused by debris floating in the ether between the planets. They were, every one of them, wrong."

"What, then?" Salisbury asked.

"The sun," Strong said, "the natural dynamo that is at the center of our solar system, and which exerts a powerful but unseen influence upon the earth. An English astronomer named Carrington, whose hobby was to daily count the number of spots on the sun, noted on the first day of the manifestation a series of spectacular geomagnetic explosions that sent waves of electro-magnetism hurtling toward our planet. A similar helio storm has not occurred until, apparently, now."

"That is a fantastic story," Lawson said.

"All the more fantastic because it has been proven true by science," Strong said. "If only we could harness the electro-motive power of the aurora borealis, mankind would have a limitless source of cheap power. It is something I understand that Mr. Edison is hard at work on. Until that time, we must make do with our galvanic cells."

"What about the odd messages?" I asked.

"Yes," Salisbury said. "I'm sure I copied the text correctly."

"Bah! Your mind is tricking you into making sense of the noise," Strong said. "It is a perfectly understandable human trait, but perfectly wrong. Somewhere in your brain, long was there that biblical verse and that message about Vicksburg tucked away, just waiting to bubble to the surface."

"I don't believe both Salisbury and Mackie would have the same bubble just waiting to froth up," I said.

"Coincidence," Strong said. "It means nothing."

"And the black train?"

"I saw no other train," Strong said.

"But sir," Salisbury said. "We all of us saw it. And heard the cursed thing."

"It wasn't there."

"Another trick of the mind?" I asked.

"Did you see it?" Strong asked. "Up close?"

"I had my eyes closed," I said. "But that was only because I was afraid it would ram us. I saw it approaching, however, and then watched as it rumbled off to the east."

"Did you see it distinctly?"

"Nothing about it was distinct, except the threat it posed."

"And do you have any expertise in railway matters?"

"None," I said.

It was true. Not knowing the names or purposes, I struggle to describe even the simplest of railway things. And the extent of my ignorance didn't end there, but in some cases it was willful ignorance. Guns are an enigma to me, and that's the way I like to keep it, because you can't write a poem or sing a song or paint a picture with a gun. I am as dumb as a sack of hair when it comes to banking and commerce, and the stock market to me seems as rigged in favor of the house as the faro and dice games in any frontier saloon. Confidence schemes I understand, because it had been my profession for so long, and I had lived with greed and obsession and guilt. But the everyday world of double-entry bookkeeping, of regular hours and customary wages, of hearth and home and pudding after dinner, was as alien to me as the sands of the Levant.

"I wouldn't expect a woman to know about such things," Strong said.

"Nor pudding," I said.

"What?"

"It's not important," I said.

"Need I say more?" Strong asked, and gave Lawson and Salisbury a fraternal look.

Delaney came with the tea then, two steaming cups on a lacquered tray. He placed them on the desk before us. I turned the handle of mine around and brought it beneath my nose, breathing in the rejuvenating aroma. The events of the night had left me somewhat more fatigued than I had realized.

"Thank you, Delmar," I said.

"Mr. Delaney, if you please," Strong corrected. "There is no reason to be overly familiar."

"Of course. What was I thinking?"

I sipped my tea. It was hot and strong and some expensive brand that I was never likely to have again. The general manager did not touch his cup.

"How long do you think the phenomenon will tie up the lines, sir?" Salisbury asked.

"A few hours," Strong said. "Back in fifty-nine, as I recall, the longest stretch in which it was impossible to operate was only eight hours. The railway will be back up and running by dawn. Until that time, we will remain on this siding, and monitor the circuit until normalcy returns."

"What if it doesn't?" I asked. "What if this is, from now and forever, the new normality?"

"A preposterous thought," Strong said, then

laughed with derision. Then he turned sober. "It would be the end of the civilized world that men have built. No telegrams, no railway schedules, no immediate news from any farther than your backyard. The stock markets would be paralyzed. The security of the country would be jeopardized. Why, we would be thrown back to the unimaginably primitive days before 1844, when Professor Morse announced his wondrous device with that memorable message—"

"*What hath God wrought*," I said.

"Precisely," Strong said. "We would be limited once again to communication at the speed of the fastest ship or horse, instead of at the speed of the lightning bolt."

"Things might be better in some ways," I said.

Strong shook his head.

"Progress always moves forward, young lady," he said. "You can no more stop the forward movement of man's ingenuity than you could stop the sun in its course. Both are ordained."

"As you like," I said. "Now that I have had my lecture, would you be kind enough to explain why you wanted to speak with me?"

"To give you my thanks, of course," Strong said. His left hand rested on the table, and with his fingertips he was gently turning the cup on its saucer. Still, he made no move to actually drink the tea.

"That would be pleasant," I said.

"Pardon?"

"Meaning I am still waiting."

He cleared his throat.

"I am grateful."

"You're welcome," I said.

"Of course, we should discuss the matter of your reward. Thirty dollars should be sufficient. Mr. Delaney, please gather the required funds."

"Yes, sir," the boy said. He placed a cash box on the table, unlocked it with a key on his watch chain, and rummaged inside. "Um, I'm afraid our expenses in New Mexico were rather higher than expected. There are no gold eagles left. I have only greenbacks . . . no, wait. I have silver dollars."

"Thirty silver dollars?"

"You would be required to sign the customary agreement," Strong said.

"Agreement?"

"A simple contract," Delaney said. "That you would keep your dealings with the railway confidential, including anything you may have witnessed tonight, from the time you set foot in our depot to, well, now."

"For how long would this silence last?"

"It would be irrevocable."

Slowly, I sipped my tea.

"For thirty pieces of silver."

"Yes," Delaney said.

"Gentlemen," I said. "I must decline."

Strong harrumphed.

"The biblical allusion alone is enough to make me wary," I said. "But the promise of silence is simply unacceptable. I have made my career chronicling the otherworldly things that intrude upon our otherwise rational lives, and I have the feeling that taking your thirty dollars would prevent me from pursuing a line of inquiry that promises to be personally more satisfying."

"What could be more satisfying than money?" Strong demanded.

"Where on the list do I begin?" I asked. "Love and friendship and creativity and learning. Helping troubled souls with unfinished business. Prairie dogs. Solving a mystery."

I finished my tea, then carefully placed my cup on its saucer.

"Miss Wylde," Strong said. "There is no mystery here, only superstition."

I took a ten-cent piece from my vest and placed it on the table.

"What's that?" he asked.

"For the tea," I said. "Just so that there is no misunderstanding. We are square."

5

It was a short walk back to Dodge, where I found the westbound freight safely on the siding beside the depot, and Doc McCarty waiting for me on the platform. He was sitting on a bench, legs stretched and ankles crossed, hands behind his head. Beside him on the bench was the telegraph key that had started the trouble.

"Earp spoke to you?"

"Briefly," McCarty said. "Enough to set me at ease that you were safe."

I motioned toward the train on the siding.

"Any trouble?"

"It required some persuasion," he said. "The engine driver relented just in time, because not two minutes after the freight was sided, a dark train flew past on the main line."

"We saw it as well."

"Mackie and the freight crew were badly frightened," McCarty said. "They did not expect it, nor did they recognize it. Some said it was a ghost train, and swore it was crewed by the dead."

"It seemed solid enough to me," I said. "It very nearly struck us, and had that occurred, I'm sure I would be quite solidly dead. Did you get a good look at the interloper?"

"It was dark and fast and silent," he said. "Its appearance was disquieting, but I saw no indication of any spectral hands on the throttle or brake."

"And the telegraph lines?"

"Still clogged with gibberish," he said.

I recounted my conversation with the general manager aboard the *Ginery Twitchell*. McCarty listened patiently, and had a few questions of a scientific nature about the helio storms, which I could not answer.

"Perhaps it will clear by morning," McCarty said.

I smiled.

"Let us hope," I said.

But it wasn't hope that tugged at my guts.

"Here," he said, handing me the key. "You said you'd take this, and Mackie's going to hold you to it."

I said good night to McCarty, then walked down the street to the agency. Calder was inside, with his boots up on his desk, the toes so close to the lighted lamp I was afraid he would knock it over.

"You left the door unlocked," he said.

"There was some excitement."

"I've heard," he said. "And seen the lights in the sky. It is all mighty queer."

"Yes," I said, opening the bottom drawer of the desk and dropping the key inside.

"What's that?"

"A hunk of brass that speaks for the dead," I said, easing myself into my chair. "A haunted telegraph key. Does the phrase 'Avail Speedwell' mean anything to you?"

"Are you speaking English?"

"I'll take that for a no," I said. "It's on the telegraph key, Jack."

"You were in no danger?" he asked.

"Nothing to speak of."

"Whenever you say that, Ophelia, it makes me nervous."

"I am in one piece, Jack," I said.

"And I am glad. Have you found a new case?"

"A mystery, perhaps, but no more," I said.

Briefly, I described the events of the night.

"Mackie is a nervous fellow," Calder said. "He might have misinterpreted that message about Hopkins being murdered at Florence. As for the dark train, who knows? Considering the confusion with the telegraph service and the operating schedules, a renegade train seems likely."

There passed a few moments of silence between us.

"Earp walked down the tracks with you."

"I told you he did."

More silence.

"Did he act peculiar?"

"What do you mean by 'peculiar'?"

"Strange, I reckon," Calder said. "*Bold* would be a better word."

"You mean, was he forward with me?" I said. "No, he assumed no liberties, and I offered him none. I do not understand the fuss that Marshal Earp generates in this town. Is it his looks? I have seen no sign that he is in any way exemplary, and he displayed tonight no special dash or daring."

"He is a good man in a tight spot."

"Possibly," I said. "But his choice of friends is questionable."

"The dentist?"

"Among other things, I understand."

"Holliday *is* strung different."

"I will rely on your word for it," I said. "And Jack—are you jealous that Earp walked with me down the tracks?"

Calder laughed.

"Jealous?" he asked. "Now, there's a rare idea. I've never had call to be jealous of any man. It is a weak emotion for weak men. A jealous man skulks, while a confident man acts."

"Nice speech," I said. "Been reading Horatio Alger again?"

"No," he said, his feelings riled. "While *Ragged Dick* is a very instructive book, it is a book for boys. There's nothing about jealousy in it. My thoughts on the subject are my own."

"If it were anyone else protesting so strongly that he was not jealous," I said, "I would be inclined to think that he was indeed filled with envy."

"It's good then that you don't think that of me."

"We are in perfect agreement," I said.

"We could not be more so," he said.

Not long after, Calder bid me a chilly good night. I locked the door behind him, then took my lamp and went to the stairs. Eddie, who had been asleep on the newel post, gave a start. He flapped his wings in protest and made an ugly cawing sound in his throat, and as I passed I apologized for disturbing him.

Unlike my previous room at the Dodge House, the rented room above the agency almost had the appearance of home. There were deep blue velvet curtains over the window, an oak gothic revival table with a wash basin and mirror, and a bed with a violet cover and six goose down pillows. I placed the lamp on the table and sat on the bed.

As I unbuttoned my vest, I saw Horrible Hank's glowing green face leering at me from the mirror on the table. The oval mirror was about the size of a pie tin, and mounted in a wooden frame that turned, so that I could face the glass down if needed. I had long ago given up on hanging mirrors on the walls, in favor of a little privacy.

"Don't mind me," Hank said. "Continue."

"Stop it," I said. "Or I'll turn you face down."

"I'll tell you a joke," he said.

His hair and clothes were gently billowing. Most times, he seemed to be standing in a windstorm, but now it seemed as if he were floating in cold green water.

"No," I said.

"But I have a new one."

"How can you have a new one?" I asked.

"I don't know."

"Perhaps your brother is sending you material."

He thought about that for a moment, then shook his head.

"Sam's not that funny," he said.

I reached for the mirror.

"No!" he said.

"Then get on with it, Hank."

"All right. Are you ready?"

"Now, Hank."

"Here goes. Ahem. A young couple are engaged to be married, but some weeks before the wedding they are killed in a tragic accident—"

"What kind of accident?"

"It doesn't matter what kind of accident."

"I think it matters what kind of accident."

"Would it kill you to just listen for once?"

"I'm sorry. Go ahead."

"This young couple dies in a *tragic* and completely *inexplicable* accident a few weeks before the wedding. Next thing they know, they find themselves standing at the Pearly Gates. Saint Peter welcomes them, as is customary, gives them their golden harps, and says their mansions are ready."

Hank giggled.

"The couple thanks old Saint Pete for all of the loot, but naturally they're disappointed because they were looking forward to being married. So they ask, 'Is it possible to get hitched in heaven?' Pete scratches his head and says he doesn't know, nobody has ever asked before. He tells them to wait there while he finds the answer. So they wait."

Hank put his chin in his hand and drummed his fingers, signifying waiting.

"After a year, Pete returns and says that yes, it is indeed possible to get married in heaven. Overjoyed, the couple embraces."

Hank hugged himself.

"But then the woman pauses. Being the smarter of the two, and a stickler for logic, she asks the obvious question. 'If marriage is possible in heaven,' she asks, 'then what about divorce?'"

Hank's eyes grew large with barely contained mirth.

"But Saint Pete just rolls his eyes and throws up his hands. 'It took me a year to locate a preacher up here—how long do you think it will take to find a lawyer?'"

Hank laughed so hard that green tears rolled down his cheeks.

"That was hilarious," Hank said. "Why aren't you laughing?"

"Your taste in jokes has not improved," I said. "That was as bad as all the rest of them. Good night, Hank."

I turned the mirror facedown, then dressed for bed and extinguished the lamp. Then I went to the window and opened it a few inches, to get a bit of air. When I was a little girl, there was a widespread fear of sleeping with your windows open at night; the theory was that miasma emanating from the swamps and the graveyards and the night soil in the necessary houses would waft into your bedroom and make you sick. When I was thirteen or fourteen, I guessed that it might have more to do with wealth, because rich folks like my parents could afford houses where the doors and windows were shut tight, while poor folk—the kind most likely to get sick because of diet, unsanitary conditions, or lack of general medical care—rarely could afford houses that shuttered tight. And even though the British surgeon Joseph Lister had debunked the miasma theory of disease in favor of germ theory, many people across America still continued the habit of sleeping in stifling bedrooms for fear of breathing bad air.

After opening the window, I parted the curtains to look at the sky. Even looking to the south, across Front Street, I could still see wisps of red and green in the night sky, and an occasional blue arc on the telegraph wire. The freight was still sided at the station, the inside of the station was brightly lit, and someone—I presumed it to be Mackie—was sitting in the shadows on a bench on the station platform. Then I looked closer and realized it wasn't Mackie at all, but Calder. He was watching my window, because he gave me a curt wave.

I waved back, then closed the curtains.

Climbing into bed, I closed my eyes. I had been sleepy just five minutes before, but now I was wide awake. I opened my eyes and stared up into the darkness, watching the protean shapes and dark amorphous blobs, which are merely artifacts of human vision, which float before us in such conditions. After a few minutes, I got up, went back to the window, and parted the curtains.

Calder was still there.

I raised the sash.

"What are you doing?" I shouted.

"Taking a rest," he said.

"You are watching my window."

"Why would I do that?"

"Shut up!" somebody called from the hotel next door. *"Won't you let us sleep?"*

"Go home," I told Calder.

I closed the window and turned my back. I was oddly and unreasonably furious at his behavior. He had no right to spy on me, and yet he claimed some proprietary interest in my nocturnal affairs. Then I turned back and glanced through the panes, and saw that he was still sitting and watching.

"Outrageous," I said.

I fumbled on the clothes pegs behind the door and found my dark hooded knee-length cape that I wear when it is occasionally necessary to leave the room at night. I slipped on the cape and tied it in front, jammed my feet into my boots without lacing them, then felt my way down the dark stairs to the agency.

"Nevermore," Eddie cried from the newel post.

"You said it, bird."

6

I crossed to the door, lifted the latch, and was out on the street in an instant, making my way down and across to the depot. Only, Calder wasn't sitting there anymore. I stood in the street a moment, feeling foolish in my nightclothes and cape, and hoping no one would see me. Then I turned back and made for the shadows beneath the porches and false fronts on the north side of the street.

As I passed the dark windows of the Occident Saloon, two doors down from the agency, I was startled by a man who struck a match on his belt buckle and lit a cigar with it. He was leaning lazily against a red hooped water barrel, the kind that dotted every block in the case of fire, and from the glow of the match I could see that his face was hard and stubbled and that he wore a bowler hat tilted forward over his brow.

"Good evening," he said.

I smiled, but said nothing, and tried to walk past.

He stuck out his boot.

"Where you off to in such a hurry?"

I sidestepped the offending piece of footwear.

"Stay and we can talk."

His voice was rough and confident and sounded like he belonged east of the Mississippi, but not too far east. Chicago, perhaps.

"Nonsense," I said.

He grasped the shoulder of my cape and pulled me to him.

"I said, Ophelia Wylde, we should talk."

It seemed odd that he knew my name.

"I am always willing to interview prospective clients," I said. "The agency opens at nine o'clock, mostly, but sometimes as late as eleven," I said. "Considering what an active night I've had, your best chance would probably be in the afternoon. Of course, your behavior has already made me disinclined to take your case, so if I were you, I wouldn't get my hopes up."

I jerked free of his grasp.

"How sharper than a serpent's tooth is a woman with a wicked tongue."

"You've bent the quote all up," I said.

"It's in the Bible," he protested.

"That's not in the King James, you idiot. That's Shakespeare, and it's about an ungrateful child," I said. "So you've now compounded your ignorance."

He drew a gun from inside his coat.

"You think you're smarter than everybody else, don't you?"

"No," I said. "Sadly, I am not smarter than most people. I have some talents that I attempt to use to my best advantage, but there are plenty of people who are smarter and more talented than I am. I'm sure you have admirable qualities yourself that are not, at this moment, apparent."

He drew back the hammer of the gun until it locked.

"Be still for one moment," he said.

"I tend to talk when I'm scared," I said. "And right now, you're scaring the daylights out of me. What do you want?"

"Shut up," he said, and shoved the barrel of the gun into my ribs.

I was quiet.

"You're going to turn down the alley between the buildings, with me right behind you," he said.

"And then what?"

"Never you mind," he said.

"We'd be more comfortable at the agency."

"Just go," he said.

"All right," I said softly, taking a cautious step forward. The gun pressed against my side, and I took a few more steps, wondering how much longer I had to live. Once we were in the darkness of the alley, I stumbled along, unsure of my footing amid the broken bottles and other debris that had been thrown there.

"Keep going," he said.

"It's dark," I said.

Then I tripped on one of my laces and fell.

The moment I struck the ground, there was the deafening roar of a pistol shot.

I cried out in terror, sure that I had been murdered.

There were two more shots, and then another, all in quick succession, and I realized that the shots were coming from several yards down the alley. My abductor was staggering back, toward Front Street, and as he reached the light I could see that he was holding one arm tight across his chest, but still grasping the pistol with his other hand.

"Stop!"

It was Calder, advancing out of the darkness. He touched my shoulder as he walked past, his large gun at the ready, his eyes on the stricken man in the bowler hat.

"Drop the pistol," I heard Wyatt Earp call from the street.

Earp was walking toward him from the west, gun held low but ready.

The man in the bowler turned sideways to regard this new threat, then attempted to bring his gun up.

Earp fired.

The bullet struck the man in the throat.

He dropped the gun and fell to his knees. The gun discharged when it struck the ground, and the bullet ricocheted from a hoop on one of the fire buckets and made a wicked zinging sound.

Blood spewed from the man's throat, squirting

in time to his heartbeat. The man clawed at the wound, looking absurdly as if he were trying to loosen his collar, and the bowler hat fell to the street.

"Are you all right?" Calder asked me.

I had been following behind him, and he noticed I was limping.

"Turned my ankle," I said.

"Stay put," he said.

The man had toppled over now, still clutching his geysering throat, and his hands were wet with blood. Earp walked over and kicked the gun out of his reach.

Calder knelt down, but kept his own gun ready.

"You're dying," Calder said. "You're shot twice in the brisket and once in the windpipe, and you're bleeding out pretty quick. You might as well make a clean account of things and tell me who you're working for."

The man's eyes were wide in terror.

"What about your name?"

The man tried to speak, but just managed a horrible wet sound.

"Dammit, Wyatt, why'd you have to shoot him in the throat?"

"Wasn't like I had the time or the light to take real careful aim," Earp said.

The gunshots had summoned Mackie from the station, and he was watching timidly from a few yards away. A few curious others were milling about in the street, and a few lamps were now lit in the storefronts.

"Isn't there anything you can do for him?" I asked.

"Yeah," Calder said. "Let him die."

"Why?"

"He was going to kill you, Ophelia."

"This isn't right," I said, limping toward the man. "We can't just."

Calder held me back.

"You know how sometimes a wolf is the most dangerous when it's in a trap and dying?" Calder asked. "It's the same here."

"But he's not an animal," I said, afraid I was going to cry.

"Mackie, go fetch Doc McCarty," Earp said.

The telegrapher dashed off down the street.

The left sleeve of Earp's white shirt was dripping with blood.

"You're hurt, too."

"Damn it," Wyatt said, noticing it for the first time. "Must've been that damned ricochet what stung me." He flexed his hand several times. "It's nothing, because I can still move my arm and my fingers."

"Doc still needs to look at it," I said. "Calder, do something."

Calder sighed and handed his gun to Earp, who now held a gun in each hand. Then Calder pulled a kerchief from his pocket and pressed it against the man's throat, trying to stem the flow of blood.

"Doc better hurry," Calder said. "It's frothy."

Calder applied more pressure.

The man's hands loosened and fell to his sides, and his eyelids fluttered.

"Careful," Earp said. "You're strangling him."

"Then tell me how to do it otherwise."

Calder repositioned his hands.

"There," he said. "I can feel—"

The man drew a silver dagger from his belt with a bloody right hand.

"Knife," Wyatt said.

Calder sprang back as the point of the knife came in an arc toward his gut. The blade missed, but narrowly. Calder, who was now standing, pinned the man's wrist to the ground with the heel of his right boot.

"Want me to finish him?" Wyatt asked.

The man writhed for a moment, then went limp.

"No need," Calder said. "It's the end of him."

"How can you tell?" I asked.

"Both wolves and men stop bleeding when they die."

Then McCarty came, carrying a lamp and in his nightshirt, and confirmed what we already knew. He looked at Wyatt's wound, and said it wasn't very deep, but that it would be wise to wash it out with carbolic acid. Then McCarty insisted on looking at my ankle, and, after feeling it, declared that it wasn't broken.

Wyatt reached down and scooped the dented bowler from the street. He glanced inside, then removed a card and asked McCarty to bring the lamp over so that he could read it.

"Says his name was Frank Blackmar," he said. "A Pinkerton man."

That would explain the Chicago accent, but little else. The Pinkertons often worked for the railways, but from what I knew they were more associated with the Rock Island than the Santa Fe.

"Sometimes people carry false credentials," Calder said. "Everybody's heard of the Pinkertons, so that would buy some influence. We can send a telegram tomorrow to Chicago asking them to confirm his identity."

"No, we can't," I said. "The wires are down, remember?"

Wyatt tossed the hat next to the body of the mysterious gunman.

"Somebody should call Mitford," he said.

"I'm glad you're not badly hurt, Wyatt."

As soon as I spoke the words, I realized that I had stopped thinking of him as Earp the moment he was wounded.

"Any idea what this man was after?" Calder asked.

"Not the faintest," I said.

"Do you think it could be connected to your newfound railway friends?"

"I can't imagine," I said. "I did not care for Strong, but there seems no advantage for the railroad to have me killed. No one could have predicted the circumstances that led to my meeting with Strong on the *Ginery Twitchell,* and I seemed the least informed of anyone about the atmospheric phenomenon and the disruption of the telegraph lines."

"Come on, Ophelia," Calder said. "I'll help you get home."

"I think I can manage."

"I'd feel better knowing you were home safe," Calder said.

"So would I," Wyatt said. "Go with him, Ophelia."

I relented.

"Calder," I said. "You were watching because you knew something wasn't right. And you, too, Wyatt."

"Not me," Wyatt said. "I was just coming down the street rattling doors when the fireworks started. It didn't take long to figure the odds. Jack, stop by the office tomorrow so you can give me a statement and we can make it all square and legal for the judge."

"How did you know?" I asked Calder.

"I didn't," he said. "But the man seemed to be hanging around the block for some reason, and I knew you had been leaving the door to the agency unlocked. Then, after shouting at me from your open window, you came downstairs and made it pretty easy for him to hustle you into the alley."

"So you heard all of it."

"Sure," Calder said.

"You waited a long time before doing anything."

"I was waiting for him to say what he was after," Calder said.

"You *waited*?"

"Yes."

"What if I hadn't fallen?" I asked. "You wouldn't

have had a clear shot. He had the gun jammed so tight into my side, that he certainly would have killed me before you had a chance."

"I knew something would happen," Calder said. "Something always does."

Somehow I didn't find Calder's faith in luck very comforting.

7

Safe, with the agency door locked and my bedroom window shut, I tumbled into bed and fell into a dreamless sleep. I slept far too late the next day, not rising until after nine. As I dressed, I knew that Calder was already at work downstairs, because I could smell coffee.

I was still yawning as I walked downstairs and took a cup from the sideboard.

"Good morning," Calder said, looking up from his paperwork.

I mumbled something in reply as I filled the cup from the enamel coffeepot on the stove. Then I found my way to my own desk and sat down, both hands clasping the cup.

"Wild night, wasn't it?"

"Any word on our mysterious Mr. Blackmar?"

"There was no other identification on him, other than inside the hat," Calder said. The dented bowler was resting on the corner of the desk. "Doc was thorough in his inspection of the body, and Mitford has him on ice next door."

I made a face.

"Well, can't let him rot before somebody comes to claim him."

"What are you working on?"

"Warrants served so far this month," he said. "It's usually a little lean after the cattle season, but this year has been surprisingly busy. Ford County residents appear determined this year to keep pace with the state's larger municipalities in terms of felonies committed and bonds jumped."

"And I thought we would just have to settle for being proud of our new school building," I said.

I sipped some more coffee while Calder scribbled away with his pen.

His face said there was something wrong, but I knew from experience that he would do just about anything to avoid talking about his feelings. There was no real need to work on the accounts this morning, I knew, as the court had recently settled up with him for returning bail jumpers during the previous ninety days. Whatever he was doing—and he had an odd habit sometimes of making lists and figuring averages, particularly when following the scores of the local baseball teams—I knew it was just busywork to keep him from thinking about something else.

And it wasn't hard to guess what that something else might be.

"Calder," I said.

"Yes?"

"Does it bother you having killed men?"

He returned the pen to the inkwell and blotted the ledger.

"It's not something I think about," he said.

"I don't believe you," I said.

Calder swiveled in his chair and looked at me.

"If Blackmar hadn't of been put down," he said, "it would have been the end of you. Why are you feeling guilty about it?"

"I'm not," I said. "The violence was horrific, and I would have liked to have been spared that, but you and Wyatt were clearly justified in the use of force."

"I am in hopes the judge will see it that way."

"How many men have you killed?"

"I don't count," he said.

"Of course you do. You keep incessant lists of everything, from the number of warrants you've served this month, compared to the same time last year, to the number of runs at bat the pitcher of the Red Stockings can expect on any given day. So, tell me."

"Seven," he said. "That counts Blackmar."

"How did the first one make you feel?"

"Rotten," he said. "Just like I do now."

"I'm glad you feel rotten," I said. "I don't think I'd like you if you didn't."

Calder rubbed the back of his ear.

"The old days were pretty wild," he said. "Back when Dodge was young, and there wasn't any police force here, and the nearest law was at the fort, five miles away. If you think Dodge is wide open now, you should have seen it then, because it was hell on greased skids."

"But there was the Committee of Vigilance," I said.

"We had to do something," he said. "So we formed our own police force, or at least our own idea of what it should be, and in the winter of 1873 we got our start by breaking up a saloon fight in which a couple of hands were killed. They deserved it, I guess. Then a month later, we chased out of town a buffalo hunter by the name of McGill who had been shooting out the lights in town just for the hell of it, and when he pulled his long gun on us, we killed him. It was me and Jimmy Hanrahan and John Scott—Scotty—doing most of the shooting, both times. The other bad elements in town got the message clear enough, and things settled down."

He paused.

"And then," he said, "some members of the committee began to enjoy the power we had. We had cleaned up the town, sort of, but then we started acting like the very people we had wanted to drive out in the first place. It doesn't take but a little power to give a man a powerfully big head, and we had a bad case of it. We walked around like we owned the place—which, in truth, we really did."

"But you didn't act that way."

"Not at first," he said. "But I came around soon enough. I began taking a free drink and that occasional cigar and a meal every once in a while, and after just a couple of weeks I began to expect those things. Felt like I was owed them, somehow, but the truth is that I was just another bully."

"That doesn't sound like you."

"You wouldn't have spoken to me then."

"What happened?"

"Things continued on like that for a while," he said. "Then the cattle season came and the town started growing and the free drinks poured down on us like water. In early June, some members of the committee stole a mule team and wagon belonging to the colonel's manservant. When an orderly ran out to stop the theft, Scotty killed one of the mules for spite. I don't even remember why we wanted the wagon. It wasn't even loaded."

"You were there?"

"And as drunk as the rest," he said. "It seemed like grand sport at the time, taking the wagon, but when the mule was killed, it wasn't having fun anymore—it was just madness. It never occurred to us that we were doing exactly the same thing that we had run others out of town for, or forced confrontations that got them killed. After the killing of the mule, we were a mob. I remember my gun in my hand, ready. Didn't know what I was ready for, but I was ready. That gun was going to be fired."

He paused and stared out the window, as if he were seeing it again.

"The colored man, Taylor, confronted us," he said. "He objected rather strenuously to the killing of the mule, and said we should be ashamed of ourselves, and that there would be hell to pay

when the colonel learned of what had happened.
And then the mob just opened fire."

"He was killed?"

"Badly wounded," Calder said. "I sobered up
then, just as if somebody had doused me with
cold water, and me and a few others carried
Taylor to the nearest drugstore, run by a man
named Fringer, who dressed the wounds. But
after I left the drugstore, a mob led by Scotty
broke in and dragged the colored man screaming into the street, where they shot him dead."

"Good Lord."

Calder rubbed at the ink stain on his forefinger, from where he had gotten a bit careless
while making his lists in the ledger. It occurred to
me that the forefinger was his trigger finger.

"But you didn't shoot, did you?"

"I don't remember shooting," he said. "But
afterward, when I examined my revolver, there
were three empty chambers. So I must have fired
half a cylinder at something. It's possible I just
fired into the air, because there was a lot of that.
Or I could have helped kill the mule. I remember thinking at the time that a dead mule was
ever so funny."

I looked down at the large and shining gun in
the holster on his hip.

"But there's a chance I may have shot Taylor,"
he said.

"Is that the same gun you had then?"

"No," he said. "Back then it was an old Army
model cap-and-ball. Cartridge guns were quite

new, and expensive. But I got rid of the gun soon after because I couldn't stand the feel of it."

He cleared his throat and took a swallow of his coffee.

"I swore to myself that I'd never get that drunk again," he said. "At least not while wearing heavy iron."

"That seems wise," I said. "Did anything happen to this Scotty?"

"A warrant was sworn out for his arrest, but he hid for two days in the ice house behind the Peacock Saloon, and then lit out," Calder said. "Never has been seen since, at least not around here. He was the only one indicted."

"What happened to the rest?"

"Still here, most of them. Hanrahan, for example. He led some buffalo hunters to the panhandle in June of 1874, and that resulted in the Second Battle of Adobe Walls with the Comanches, but he survived that to return to Dodge. Right after the death of Taylor, I packed up and went back to Presidio County—"

Calder had told me the story before, but in abbreviated form. I knew he had had a family in Texas, and that their wagon had been attacked by the Comanches at Sharp's Creek at about the time of the second Adobe Walls battle.

"You didn't tell me you were in Dodge before."

"It's a story I'm ashamed of," he said. "I had left Sarah and the boy in Texas. I had come up to Dodge looking for work, and found whiskey. That was easy, because I was the enforcer at Tom

Sherman's barroom. After the killing of Taylor, I returned to my home in Presidio County."

On an adventure the year before, Calder had told me the story of how his wife and child were killed by a renegade band of Quanah Parker's band of Comanches—and how he had tracked down and killed three of them, which began his career as a bounty hunter.

"After Sarah and Johnnie were gone," he said, "all that had held promise for me in Texas was dead. I drifted back to Dodge and became a bounty hunter, because hunting people down and killing them seemed my only talent. And now that I was sober, I was damned good at it. The men I hunted deserved it, murderers and rapists. Every one of them, I thought, had taken their share of women and children, and if they resisted being brought back to stand trial, they deserved to die. I also discovered that the less one is concerned about one's own life, or about leaving a widow and orphans, the more cool and calculated one could become."

"Were you hoping that you yourself would be killed?"

"I simply did not care," he said. "I hated myself because I could not stand the precious time I had wasted, away from my own family. It wasn't just the Comanches that had taken them away from me, Ophelia. I had made the choice myself."

"You went back to them."

"Too late," he said. "If only I could have had just one of those days back that I had squandered drinking and acting the fool, things would have been different. But of course, it never works that way. We are saddled with debts that we can never repay."

"How did you conquer your grief?"

"Wouldn't say I conquered it," he said. "It was more like a cease-fire."

"What changed?"

"Dodge changed, for one," he said. "A regular police force was established. There were fewer warrants to serve and, with some exceptions, the truly bad men began to avoid town."

"There's still a vigilance committee," I said. "You've told me."

"There is," he said. "But it's not needed like it once was."

He cleared his throat, picked up his pen, and carefully dabbed the excess ink from the tip into the well before studiously returning to his lists.

"Perhaps," he said, his eyes still on the rows of figures, "it never really was needed at all."

8

I drank another cup of coffee and had a slice of toast and pondered Calder's history with the vigilance committee. The events he described were just four and one-half years distant, but things change fast on the frontier, and Dodge had transformed itself from a burgeoning hamlet with a few wooden buildings and many tents to an established, if not yet entirely civilized, municipality on the hundredth meridian, where the West begins. In my sixteen months here, I had come to think of it not as the edge of the world, but as the edge of the world with a few amenities.

At half-past ten, Eddie—who was sitting atop Lincoln's head and watching the business of the agency with his characteristic calm—announced the arrival of strangers at our door by stretching his wings and emitting an evil-sounding chuckle. I looked, and a shadowy cluster of men had appeared on the board sidewalk outside the agency door. This was followed by a curt knock.

"It's open," I called.

That dandy Delaney held the door for General Manager Strong, who strode into the agency with all the gravity of a captain walking onto the deck of a ship. That rubbed me the wrong way, because the agency was *my* ship. Behind him were Salisbury and Lawson, the telegraph men, and another man whom I had not seen before.

Eddie beat his wings and, I imagine, swore in raven language.

"What in heaven's name is that thing?" Strong asked.

"That is not a thing," I said. "His name is Eddie, and he is a free raven and a valued member of the agency. Eddie, say hello to the general manager."

"*'Bells, bells, bells!'*"

"He is quite fond of quoting Poe," I said.

"A talking raven," Strong said. "Have we entered Barnum's?"

"No humbug here, I assure you."

There followed a round of introductions, so that Calder could know the names of our visitors. The new man—who looked to be perhaps forty-five years old, with a bulge beneath his coat that was obviously a firearm—was introduced as J.H. Grunvand. He clasped a book under one arm. Calder dragged a chair from the back for Strong. The rest could stand, the general manager said.

Then I asked: "Where's Engineer Skeen?"

"At the engine, as his contract requires," Strong said.

I whistled.

"Let's see, that means he's been on duty for twelve or fourteen hours?" I asked. "I'm sure that's not in his contract."

"Exigent circumstances, miss," Strong said. "Exigent circumstances."

"So, the trouble on the wire hasn't cleared up?"

"Afraid not," Salisbury said. "If anything, it's worse."

"Still all Bible verses and antique messages?"

Neither Salisbury nor Lawson dared answer.

"Ah," I said. "Still think this has a natural explanation?"

"I don't know," Salisbury stammered.

"I'm glad you gentlemen are here," Calder said. "We had a mystery of our own last night that you might be able to help us clear up. A man was shot while attempting to murder Ophelia."

"I am so very dearly sorry to hear that," Strong said, with no sadness in his eyes. "Did you shoot your assailant in self-defense, Miss Wylde?"

"No," I said. "I am religious in my abhorrence of guns."

"I shot him," Calder said. "Helped by one of our town marshals. The only identification was found in this hat."

Grunvand stepped forward.

"Frank Blackmar."

Calder said that it was, and asked him how he knew.

"I recognize the hat," Grunvand said. "We were partners. I am sad to think he is dead."

"My condolences," I said. "Does that mean you're a Pinkerton as well?"

Grunvand smiled.

"Yes," he said. "I am a Pinkerton man. As a matter of fact, I have brought something as a kind of calling card."

He held out the book to Calder.

"Don't assume I'm in charge around here," Calder said. "This is an equal partnership. But when it comes to books, she's the boss."

A little flustered, Grunvand offered me the book.

"Just published last year," he said.

It was a handsome book, bound in green cloth and having the Pinkerton never-sleeping eye on the cover.

"*The Spiritualists and the Detectives*," I said, reading the cover. "By Allan Pinkerton."

"Part of a series of wonderful and true detective stories by our chief," Grunvand said. "This year's title is *Strikers, Communists, Tramps, and Detectives.*"

I was familiar with the books. They were something short of wonderful and not even in the same state as true. Pinkerton—if, in fact, he did write them himself—had the annoying habit of changing names and locations to protect the identities of his clients. But it wasn't that that ultimately made me throw the book across the room, aiming for the stove but hitting the bookcase behind instead, rocking the bust of Lincoln and making Eddie screech his displeasure; no, it was a combination of a dreadful writing style, a preaching and patronizing tone, and the many untruths woven throughout. Organized labor, unconventional lives, progressive political philosophies, and open-minded religious attitudes, according to Pinkerton, all posed the gravest threats yet encountered by hard-working Americans. Particular hate was reserved for the Brotherhood of Locomotive Engineers.

I returned the book to Grunvand.

"I've already read this one, thank you."

Calder picked up the bowler and brushed the felt.

"Tell me," he said, "why your Blackmar would want my partner dead."

"That is especially troubling," Grunvand said. "I know of no reason."

"How long had you both worked for the Santa Fe?"

"I'm afraid we can't divulge—"

"Oh, for God's sake," Strong exclaimed. "We're burning through seventy-five thousand dollars a day with the line tied up. Tell the man what he wants to know."

"Three weeks," Grunvand said.

"Why were you hired?"

Grunvand looked at Strong.

Strong waved his hand impatiently.

"There had been some irregular business that we were called to investigate," Grunvand said.

"It seemed silly to me, at first. Crews from the Argentine yards to Newton were complaining of a ghost train."

"A black train."

"Yes, a short funeral train with no markings," he said. "Always at night. Some swore they saw it crewed by ghouls, with skeletons trotting alongside with coffins on their backs."

"Sounds like the stories told about the phantom funeral train of President Lincoln," I said.

"Yes, but Lincoln's train was never east of the Mississippi," Grunvand said. "And, of course, there's the scientific fact that phantoms and ghosts simply do not exist."

Calder laughed.

"I saw something similar," I said. "Last night, from aboard the *Ginery Twitchell*. I had the impression that it was very real."

"Impossible," Grunvand said. "There is simply no way an unscheduled train could traverse the line, without orders, and not collide with other locomotives or rolling stock, or be derailed by a switch turned the wrong way."

"So, what is this train?" Calder asked.

"I don't know."

"You're a mite short on answers, aren't you?" Calder asked. "Why don't you tell us why you're here, because I haven't heard a reason yet."

"We've come to engage your services," Strong said.

"You want to hire us," Calder said.

"More than that," I said. "They need our help."

"Well, yes," Strong said.

"To solve the mystery," I said.

"To help us correct our negative cash flow condition," Strong said.

"And that would require us to solve the mystery," I said.

"I don't care how you do it," he said. "Frankly, I don't believe in all this hoodoo about ghosts and spirits, and I still think there is a rational explanation for what seem to be undelivered messages on the wire."

"Undelivered?" I asked.

"Yes," Lawson said. "We took turns listening and copying messages all night, and most seem to have this in common: they appear to be undelivered messages, or lost messages, or communications that for one reason or another did not reach their intended recipient. Many of the messages include requests for forwarding, or replies that the recipient had died, or were dispatches for trains that had, well, had already met with some catastrophe. Ashtabula River was among them."

The worst disaster in American railway history had occurred a couple of years before near Ashtabula, Ohio, when a bridge collapsed and a train plunged a thousand feet into the icy river below. Ninety-two people had died. I knew something of the accident because, in my past life as a confidence woman, I pretended to have made contact with one of the victims—and was found out.

"That is curious," I said. "In my line of work, I find that revenants—"

The word did not register with Grunvand.

"Revenants," I said. "Those who return from

the dead. Revenants always have unfinished business, so it makes sense to me that ghostly telegraph messages would be somehow incomplete or otherwise unfinished."

Strong grew impatient.

"Haste, woman," he said. "Haste. Spare me your lectures on the springtime country or whatever else it is you call the other life. Deal with the here and now. We have been plunged back to the days of the Pony Express, cut off as we are from convenient communication with our headquarters in Topeka, or with the chief detective Allan Pinkerton in Chicago. We are a wagon that has thrown a wheel, and you are unfortunately the only blacksmith available."

"Yes, how unfortunate for you," I said. "Let's discuss terms."

"Terms?" Strong asked. "Where's your patriotism, Miss Wylde? The Santa Fe is America, and America needs you. Let us not sully the task at hand with a crass discussion of profit."

"Strange," I said. "I don't ever remember capitalists being afraid to discuss profit before. But let me put your mind at ease, because this agency is positively communal in its approach to profits."

"What is she talking about?" Strong asked Calder.

"We don't make a profit from our clients," Calder said. "We only charge actual expenses."

"Then how do you stay in business?"

"Through readers," I said. "In exchange for

our services, clients must agree to allow me to write a public account of their case—no matter where it leads. Our living comes from the sales, royalties, and subscriptions of the resulting books. Our daily bread is bought with the pleasure that our readers derive from sharing our adventures."

"Out of the question," Strong said. "We will deal on a confidential and cash basis. A thousand dollars should be sufficient, I think. Mr. Delaney, please write out a check in that amount, and I will sign it."

"No, thank you," I said.

"I beg your pardon?" Strong asked.

"Yes," Calder said. "Pardon?"

"We've explained the rules," I said. "You may either agree to them, or not. But the rules are not subject to negotiation. We cannot be bought."

"Ophelia," Calder said. "Would it hurt to—"

"No, Jack. Stand with me on this one."

There was a deadly pause.

"Yes," Calder said. "Ophelia is correct. We stand by our rules."

"Lunatics," Strong said.

"Perhaps," I said. "But remember, we're the only blacksmith you have."

Strong looked at Grunvand, who shrugged.

"Oh, all right," he said. "Show me the contract."

"We operate on a handshake here," Calder said.

Strong shook hands with both of us.

"What are your expense requirements?" he asked.

"Transportation," I said.

"Mr. Delaney," Strong said. "Please provide Miss Wylde with a pass that is good for our line and all connections and reciprocal agreements. That reaches from coast to coast, if need be. It is also good for overland coach operations, if they connect to our track as well."

"This is a rush job," I said. "I require the assistance of my partner, Jack Calder, and Dr. Thomas McCarty."

"The pass will prove good for yourself and up to two companions."

"And the expiration date?"

Travel was always a major obstacle. Some of our clients simply could not afford the cost of the transportation that was often necessary.

Strong sighed.

"One year," he said.

"Make it a lifetime pass and we will waive all other expenses."

Calder shot me a look of disbelief.

"For a refugee from the commune," Strong said, "you are quite a tough negotiator. Oh, all right. But for *your* lifetime only."

He directed young Delaney to make it so.

"Is there anything else?"

"No," I said. "My companions should leave within the hour for your station at Florence. Will that be possible, given the condition of the rails?"

"Not only is it possible, but it will be an express,

with no stops," Strong said. "Nothing else is running. You and your associates will be there in time for supper. Mr. Delaney will accompany you, of course."

"Of course," I said.

"Ah, Miss Wylde," Grunvand said. "I have been to the charming restaurant at the hotel—such a surprise for the weary traveler. You will enjoy the food. I can personally recommend the vinegar pie."

"It's not the food I'm interested in," I said.

"Am I to accompany them as well?" Grunvand asked Strong.

But I replied for him.

"No," I said. "You are to stay with the general manager. If there was an attempt on my life, then he may be in danger as well."

"Yes, certainly," Grunvand said. "That's what I was thinking."

I paused.

"I am sorry for the loss of your friend," I said.

"As am I," Grunvand said. "And I find it impossible to explain his actions."

"Explaining away attempted murder is never easy," I said. "Do you think the family would like his body returned to Chicago?"

"Thank you, but you have it wrong," Grunvand said. "Frank had never been to Chicago. He was from Missouri, and worked out of the St. Joseph office. The chief hired him on the basis of a recommendation from one of our longtime operatives, after he proved useful in the James-Younger affair."

"But he had a Chicago accent."

"Oh, no," Grunvand said. "His speech was rustic."

Calder stood.

"I think you'd better walk over to the furniture store and take a look at the body," Calder said. "I have a feeling the gentleman on ice over there isn't your friend at all."

9

Within the hour, Grunvand confirmed that the corpse at Mitford's was not Frank Blackmar; McCarty was summoned and agreed to accompany us to Florence; and I packed a few clothes and provisioned my well-worn leather ammunition satchel (which itself had once belonged to a murderer and was a prize from a previous case) with those things that I knew from experience would prove handy.

I spent a few minutes sitting on the stairs and talking with Eddie, who had relocated to the newel post. I told him that I was called away on a case, and that I didn't know how long I would be away, but that I would, sooner or later, return. In the meantime, I said, Mitford the Undertaker had agreed to look in on him, and make sure he had food and water. But, I said, he would not be caged inside the agency; the secret raven-sized door above the agency's main door would remain unlatched, should he wish to venture outside.

The door, which opened beneath the overhanging porch, but so high up as to be out of reach of anyone not on a ladder, was difficult to spot, even if one knew where to look. After a fire had destroyed two of the businesses along Front Street the previous summer, I began to worry that Eddie would not be able to escape should the agency catch fire, and convinced Calder to spend an afternoon fashioning and fitting the door. Calder had pasted a playing card—the Ace of Spades—on the inside of the door, as a marker so Eddie could better find his exit in case of emergency.

"Any advice for me on this one?" I asked.

Eddie ruffled his wings, a sure sign that he was anxious.

"Of course I'll be careful," I said.

By the time I gathered my things and walked to the depot, the *Ginnery Twitchell* was huffing on the main line beside the station. There was only one car behind the locomotive and tender, the railway express car. The others had been left at the old siding outside Dodge.

Young Delaney awaited me on the platform.

"Miss Wylde," he said, reaching for my bag. "May I—"

I pulled the bag out of his reach.

"Please," I said. "Allow me the dignity of carrying my own things."

"I was only trying to be a gentleman," he said.

"Most of the gentlemen I have known were not, in fact, gentle, and they hid their rapacious ways behind a cloak of civility," I said. "Merely attempt to be a human being, please."

"Of course," he said, but appeared a bit bewildered. "Miss Wylde—"

"Let's dispense with the honorifics, shall we? It will be much simpler for both of us. You may call me Ophelia, and I will call you Delmar."

"I would prefer Delaney."

"Easily granted, young Delaney."

"This is yours," he said, handing me an envelope.

I put down the bag and opened the flap. Inside were two pieces of paper.

The first was a letter, signed by Strong, that indicated I had been retained by the Atchison, Topeka, and Santa Fe, in the capacity of consulting detective, and that employees should meet any reasonable request I might have in the course of my investigation.

The other was a slip of yellow paper, about three by five inches, with the name of the railway in a flourishy script, and LIFETIME PASS in large letters. Then there was a place for my name, which was written in ink by a steady hand, and another place for the number of the pass, 03-78-07. It was signed by the general manager.

"That's it?" I asked. "I thought it might be more elaborate. Why, it is no more impressive than the advertising slips for Prickly Pear Bitters the Shinn Brothers print by the hundreds down the street at the *Dodge City Times*."

"It is worth a fortune," Delaney said. "Please

exercise some care because, if lost, it will not be replaced."

"Don't worry," I said, tucking the pass and its envelope into my satchel. "I lost a ticket once, and that was a nightmare."

"Shall we? Your friends are already aboard."

"Could I ride up front with Skeen?"

"Even your pass does not allow passengers in the cab."

The freight door in the side of the express car was open, and we stepped from the platform into the interior of the car. Calder and McCarty were sitting on a bench near the post office section of the car, and I took a chair near them. Delaney leaned out of the car and waved. Once the train began to move, he pulled the door shut and engaged the latch.

McCarty was sitting with his medical bag on his lap, his arms folded over it.

Calder had his feet stretched out in front of him, his boots crossed.

"It was strange," McCarty said, "having no news this morning, and hearing no train traffic rattle by."

"I enjoyed the peace," Calder said.

"The country could be at war," McCarty said, "and we would not know it."

"That's what was enjoyable about it."

McCarty shook his head.

"I couldn't stand this way of life for very long," he said. "It has only been a decade or thereabouts since the continent was bridged by both rail and wire, but that world seems quaint and very long ago."

"Are we any happier?" Calder asked.

"Wiser, perhaps," McCarty said.

"Neither wiser nor happier," I said. "We have more information and our affairs have become more efficient, but neither adds to the volume of the human heart. Shakespeare remains eternal, whether he is on a dusty shelf in some library, or shot like lightning from New York to San Francisco."

"Is he still eternal if all the copies of his plays rot to dust?"

It was an uncharacteristically deep question for Calder.

"Why, Jack," I said. "What an excellent question. The answer, I think, is yes—as long as someone, somewhere, is reciting a line from memory or simply recalling the story with pleasure."

McCarty told me I had put it just right, but Calder rubbed the back of his right ear and I wasn't so sure. Perhaps I was just saying what I wanted to be true.

"What about all of these undelivered messages clotting up the wires?" he said. "I don't understand where they're coming from. Are they being sent from a single source, or from everywhere?"

"Nowhere is more like it," I said.

"What do you mean?" McCarty asked.

"My guess is that it's coming from the stuff between the worlds."

"The luminiferous aether," McCarty said. "The

substance that makes the propagation of light waves possible. Something has created an aetherial tear or rift that has caused the magnificent auroras—and allowed this supernatural manifestation?"

"I think so," I said. "But it's a particular kind of rip that allows only these certain messages through, the incomplete, the lost, the undelivered. It's as if there is a sort of purgatory for messages, and somebody has thrown open the door."

"How do we close the door?" McCarty asked.

"We close the door by figuring out why somebody would want to open that door in the first place," I said. "This isn't a natural phenomenon, because it doesn't match what happened in 1859."

"And then there's the death of Hopkins," Calder said.

"The *murder* of Hopkins," McCarty said, "if Ophelia's telegraphic goblins are telling the truth."

"They're not my goblins," I said. "But yes, the death of Hopkins is the place to start. Doc, that's why I wanted you to come with us. An expert medical opinion, one that we can trust, may prove essential. Treat it as a private coroner's inquest."

"Is that legal?" McCarty asked.

"In cases where there is the consent of the family," Calder said. "But if there is no next of kin, we'll have to obtain the permission of the local prosecutor. If Hopkins has already been buried, then we'll need an exhumation order from a judge—and to get that, we'd have to show cause. Even then, judges are reluctant to disturb hallowed ground."

"We'll have to cross that bridge when we come to it," I said.

The train was going at full speed now, perhaps forty miles an hour across the prairie. The express car jostled with the motion of the rails, and the big lamp hanging over the post office desk swayed gently in time.

Delaney, who had been busy at the far end of the car, brought a tray of coffee and tea and ham sandwiches. The ham sandwiches were on thick bread, and each had a generous slice of cheese.

"I took the liberty of storing this up during our stop at Dodge," he said. "Even though Marion County is but a few hours away, we are still traveling during lunchtime. I find that I think best when my stomach's not growling, don't you, Miss Wylde?"

I gave him a stern look.

"I'm sorry," he said. "Ophelia."

"If I feed my stomach," I said, "it starves my brain."

I took only a cup of tea, while the men helped themselves to coffee and sandwiches.

"This is a fine sandwich," McCarty said, after two bites. "I especially like the spicy mustard sauce. What is it that I'm tasting? Star anise, perhaps. What do you think, Jack?"

"Don't ask me," he said, his mouth full. "My

idea of a good meal is anything that doesn't bite you back."

"What about you, Delaney?" McCarty asked. "No sandwich?"

"No, sir," he said. "The chief prefers that I bring my own meals aboard, and eat away from management and guests."

"Have a sandwich," Calder said. "We won't tell."

"No, thank you, sir," Delaney said. "Rules must be obeyed."

"Suit yourself," Calder said. "Tell me, how long have you known the Pinkerton man?"

"Grunvand? I can't say that I know him at all," Delaney said. "I met him only a few days ago. And I never was introduced to his partner, poor Frank Blackmar."

We rolled on through the October afternoon, generally following the old Santa Fe trail just north of the Arkansas River. The clusters of trees on the riverbank were already beginning to turn, patches of red and yellow signaling the arrival of fall. The sky was clear and the temperature was brisk, but not cold. About three hours into our journey, the river turned south toward Wichita, and we continued northeast toward the city of Newton.

We slowed as we passed through the city of Newton, but did not pause at the station, even though the platform was crowded with stranded passengers who attempted to flag us down by waving their arms and shouting. Some among the crowd jumped down and stormed the tracks, and I was afraid they might fall beneath the great wheels of the *Ginery Twitchell* and be sliced to bits. Engineer Skeen gave long warning blasts on the whistle, some city marshals and railway workers dragged some of the desperate people back, and somehow we managed not to kill anyone.

When it was apparent we weren't going to stop, the train was pelted with bricks, stones, and garbage. The window I was looking through was cracked by a whiskey bottle that was hurled by a young woman with wild eyes.

"It's a mob," Calder said, pulling me away from the window.

"What are they afraid of?" Delaney asked.

"They are afraid of the unknown and angry at being powerless," McCarty said. "You can't much blame them, considering they've been stranded in a strange town far from home, by circumstances they neither can control nor understand."

"No excuse for acting like animals," Delaney said.

"Crowds act with one mind," McCarty said. "And that mind is driven by animal instincts, not intellect."

I looked at Calder, and he looked away.

"We were lucky at Dodge," McCarty said, "because there's not enough passenger traffic that far west to strand many passengers. But the farther east we get, the greater the numbers will become."

A minor revelation struck me.

"That's why Strong decided to stay behind," I

said. "He was afraid to come back east for fear of the mobs."

"He did think it prudent to avoid the stations," Delaney said. "But he was not planning to remain in Dodge. If the wires do not clear by tomorrow morning, he will board an eastbound stage and make his way back to railway headquarters in Topeka."

Delaney paused.

"Perhaps I shouldn't have told you that."

"Don't worry, young Delaney. We can be trusted."

"This is a bad sign," McCarty said. "If crowds are rioting at Newton, Kansas, a railway hub on the prairie, you know things are worse in the cities. And this is just the first day. Can you imagine what things could be like in two or three days, if transportation isn't restored?"

"Allan Pinkerton's worst nightmare," I said. "An instant tramp army."

"The towns will quickly run out of food," Calder said. "I don't think the stage and freight lines could possibly haul enough to meet the demand. If you live on a farm you'll do all right, but these travelers must depend on retail operations, and with many dozens or even hundreds of passengers stranded at each point along the way, the shelves will be emptied pretty quick."

"That's a horrific thought," I said.

Soon after leaving Newton, we entered a land of rolling hills, rich fields, and many trees. It was all as peaceful as Newton was riotous.

Forty minutes later, we drew near the town of Florence. I said something to Delaney, who pulled a cord overhead, signaling Engineer Skeen. We slowed, and came to a stop on a lonely section of track.

"I think it best if we walk the rest of the way in," I said. "Let's blend into town instead of announcing ourselves by stepping off the only train running today."

"Good thinking, Ophie," McCarty said.

Delaney pulled open the freight door, sat down on the floor with his legs dangling outside, then twisted around and eased himself down the three feet to the track bed. McCarty and Calder followed, and then Calder turned, picked me up from the doorway, and placed me on the ground beside him.

Delaney gave me a questioning look.

"That was practicality," I said. "Not courtesy. My legs are shorter than theirs."

"I thought it somewhat chivalrous," Calder said.

McCarty laughed.

"Engineer Skeen and his crew will secure the train on the runabout track between the depot and the hotel," Delaney said. "We are about three-quarters of a mile away from the depot. Just a short walk on a pleasant afternoon."

We began to walk down the middle of the tracks, because the shoulders were a bit too steeply sloped to easily traverse. A quarter of a mile on, we encountered a road that intersected the tracks at an acute angle, and Delaney said we should take the road the rest of the way into town. It was welcome news, because I had quickly grown tired of adjusting my stride to step from one railway tie to another, and the dirt of the road was kinder to my feet.

We had gone only a few hundred yards when McCarty stopped.

"I'm sorry, I have become unaccustomed to exertion," he said, breathing a bit heavily. "Too many late hours and an irregular diet. This makes a poor recommendation for my capabilities as a physician, doesn't it? Please, go on. I'll catch up."

"Nonsense," I said. "We can take a rest, here, in the shade."

There was a wide grassy spot, with several oaks, and a towering cottonwood, near a stream not far from the road. On the opposite side of the stream was a field of cane sorghum, five or six feet high, mature now and awaiting harvest. Calder took his pocket knife, cut a stick of cane, and chewed on it like candy.

"Sweet," he said.

McCarty sat down on a log, and I sat next to him. Delaney found a rock.

Calder did not sit, but stood near the edge of the sorghum field, keeping an eye on the road, and chewing bits of cane and occasionally spitting out the pits.

"How do you feel?" I asked McCarty.

"I'm fine, just fine."

"You've looked better," I said.

"Pleasant spot," McCarty said, changing the subject.

"It hardly looks like Kansas, it is so pleasant here," I said.

"Oh, all of eastern Kansas is green, with rolling hills, but this area is particularly fertile, and with good water from natural springs," Delaney said.

"It reminds me of home," I said.

"Home?"

"Where I grew up," I said. "My family had an estate, just below Memphis. It was different there, more lush and with different vegetation, but at least this isn't the flat and unyielding prairie we have at Dodge."

"We're in the Flint Hills," Delaney said. "Stretches from northern Oklahoma and across Kansas, nearly to the Nebraska border. It's plenty treeless when you get away from the streams and river valleys."

"The city is named for Florence, Italy?" I asked.

"No," Delaney said. "It's named for Florence Crawford, the little girl of Samuel Crawford, our former governor. He founded the town company in 1870, after learning the Santa Fe would cross the Cottonwood here."

"You sound like a regular tour guide," I said. "Why do you know so much?"

"Because the railroad is as much in the business of selling land as it is moving people and freight," Delaney said. "The government gave the railroad twenty miles on either side of the tracks through here."

"This is not such a bad place," I said.

"Three passenger trains a day stop at Florence, and many more freights," Delaney said. "During an ordinary day, of course."

"How are you feeling, Doc?"

"Passable," he said. "Let's continue."

Calder held out his hand.

"Wait," he said, just above a whisper. "There's someone coming."

"So?" I asked.

"It looks like a renegade. Well, sort of."

"From the reservation?" I asked. "This far east?"

Calder held a finger to his lips and we waited.

We heard the clop of hoofs and the rattle of tack, and then a man riding a mule came into view, heading toward town. The mule was old, with a gray nose, and it had a straw hat, with cutouts for its pointy ears. The man wore a hat, too—a broad, floppy leather hat, with a band made of rattlesnake skin and a long turkey feather tucked into one side. Beneath the hat was a red kerchief, tied in the back. He had denim trousers and a fringed buckskin shirt that was dark with age and stains, and around his neck was a necklace made of animal bones and bird claws and porcupine quills. His face and hands were the color of walnut, but his eyes were blue, and he had a neatly trimmed white beard.

Across his saddle was a rifle. It looked very old and its octagonal barrel was brown, instead of the blue-black or shiny nickel that I was used to seeing in Dodge. There were brass tacks driven into the side of the butt in the shape of a heart, and a couple of turkey feathers and some beads hung from a loop of leather near the tip of the stick beneath the barrel.

"That's no Indian," McCarty said.

"Well, I see that now," Calder said.

As the man rode closer, he gave no indication he saw us until he had drawn abreast, and then he eased back on the reins and the mule obediently stopped in the middle of the road. The man leaned forward, and turned his head slowly, taking us all in one at a time.

"Sadie," he said to the mule. "We have some fellow pilgrims here."

"Howdy," Calder said, keeping an eye on the muzzle of the ancient rifle. "Nice piece. Fifty?"

"No," the man said. "Fifty is good for whitetail or a mulie, but a might puny for elk. Meet Old Ephraim with merely a fifty and you want to have all your prayers said and a letter to your next-of-kin in your pocket."

"Old Ephraim?" I asked.

"Grizzly," the man said, reverently.

"There are no grizzlies here," Calder said.

"There are where I'm going."

"Where's that?" Calder asked.

"The mountains," he said. "My home's in the mountains."

Calder nodded.

"What's your name?"

"Fogarty Ezekiel Fannin."

"You're Foggy Zeke?"

"Do I know you, son?"

"No, but I've heard of you," Calder said. "Along with Bridger and Carson and Jed Smith. Why don't you come down from the mule and palaver with us a spell."

"Like I said, I got business," he said. "In the mountains."

"You're riding east, Zeke," Calder said. "The mountains are behind you, some six or seven hundred miles away."

Zeke made a fearsome face.

"All good civilized people look to the east," he said. "I saw the signs, and I know the time is at hand. The entire sky lit up all night like a magic lantern show. I'm going home to the mountains, but before I go, I have to visit Granny Doom, the power doctor at Doyle Creek. And, son, my mountains are ahead of me, not behind."

Calder nodded. "What do you mean, 'power doctor'?" Calder asked.

"That one is fooling, ain't he?" Zeke asked.

"Afraid not," McCarty said. "I'm a physician myself, and I've never heard the phrase."

"Why, what kind of healer are you?" Zeke asked. "Never heard of a power doctor."

"I'm an allopath," McCarty said. His face was red and his mouth must have been dry, because he was licking his lips frequently. "I treat diseases by prescribing remedies."

"That's what the power doctor does," Zeke said. "Has a madstone, taken from the stomach of a white deer, that will suck the poison right out of you. Works for rabies and snakebite and other poisons, as long as the prayer is righteous. Do you pray?"

"Sometimes," McCarty said.

"Doc," I said, "what he's talking about is magic. Anybody who grew up in the South would know what he's talking about, or the Ozarks, or in the Appalachias. Power doctors are like yarb doctors—similar to nature healers and voodoo priests—except power doctors have a direct connection to the Almighty. A yarb doctor might be able to fix up your sour stomach with a tea made of some things picked at night in the woods. The healing is in the stuff itself. A power doctor might fix you the same tea, and make you drink it, but the healing is from the Holy Spirit. A power doctor treats the body and soul, but somebody must always pay the cost."

"Voodoo," McCarty said. "Witch doctors."

"When you pray over your patients," I said, "does it work?"

"Often enough to keep me doing it," McCarty said. "But I'm praying for the medicine to do its work, and for me to have the wisdom to know what to do, and the skill to do it."

"It's no different with power doctors," I said.

"Sounds like your past talking," McCarty said.

"I'll forgive you that, Doc, because it looks like you're pretty sick yourself."

"What do you need from the power doctor?" Calder asked.

"Sun's hot, even though the air is mild," Zeke

said, and he took off his hat, and the red kerchief beneath.

I gasped.

Delaney's eyes grew big and McCarty stared with professional interest.

There was neither skin nor hair on the greater part of the old man's head, just white bone that reflected the sunlight. We could even see the sutures where the plates of the skull met.

"Forgive my friends," Calder said.

"Don't bother me none," Zeke said, mopping his face with the kerchief.

"So the story is true," McCarty said. He was up from the log now, and standing beside the mule.

"Lost my topknot to Old Ephraim when I was thirty-six years old," he said. "It was near Coulter's Hell and I was running traps with a filthy Frenchman named Guy in the winter of forty-three. We took *beaucoup* plews, even with the Crows trying to kill us."

Zeke leaned forward in the saddle, as if to better see the past.

"But one morning while Guy was in the water putting stink on the traps, a grizzly about the size of a freight wagon came out of the mist. It was on me before I could swing my rifle, and it knocked me to the ground and got my head in its mouth. It ripped the scalp off the back of my head like it was peeling an orange. But before it had a chance to bite my head clean off, Guy was out of the water and finally to his rifle, and he put a ball down its throat. He said he missed, because he was aiming between my eyes, to put me out of my misery."

"How did you survive?" McCarty asked.

"Too mean to die," Zeke said. "The filthy Frenchman nursed me for a month, before leaving me with a woman at a Flathead village. Don't remember much of the first couple of weeks, because of the fever."

"Does it hurt?" I asked.

"Can't feel anything," he said.

"Then why do you need the power doctor?" I asked.

"Because it ain't clean," he said.

"Looks downright shiny to me," I said.

"Oh, no, there's dirt and sweat and whatnot," Zeke said. "I can't feel it, but I know it's there, and it's driving me mad. I can't scrub up there, because I can't see it, not even in a mirror, because my eyes don't swivel that way. Even if I could get an angle on it, I'm afraid I would peel away the edges of the skin I have left. So I need the power doctor to clean it, and put some ooze on it, and say a few words over me."

"So you're really talking about spiritual dirt," I said.

"When I meet Him that made me, I want to be presentable," he said. "I was presentable once, up in the mountains when both me and the world was new, but this plains living down here in the dirt has made me old and filthy."

"Looks like there are spots where the bear's teeth pierced the skull," McCarty said. "That may have been what saved you, because those holes relieved the pressure. Otherwise, you'd have died from the swelling of your brain a few days after. Can I touch it?"

"Usually it's kids that want to do that."

"But I'm a doctor."

"That's what you say."

"He's all right," I said. "His hands are clean."

"All right," Zeke said, and he leaned down.

McCarty ran his hand over the skull.

"Remarkable," McCarty said. "Thank you for obliging me."

Zeke put his hat back on.

"Wish I hadn't let my niece and that fool of a husband of hers talk me into settling down on a farm, because it's no country for me," he said. "The air is too damn thick in summer. In the winters, the snow is too damn wet. The farmhouse is too stuffy and I can't see the stars at night and nobody has any use for this child of thunder. I wish I could have spent my last days in the mountains, where I could have seen God's own light and heard His trumpet while the fools that toil on the plains were still in darkness."

"Zeke," Calder said, "it's not the end of the world."

"He's right," McCarty said.

"But the signs," Zeke said.

"Natural phenomenon," he said. "Auroras."

"I've seen the northern lights," Zeke said. "This weren't them."

"No," McCarty said, "but something similar."

"A rift, we think," I said. "In the luminiferous aether."

"Go back to your family," Calder said.

Zeke grimaced, and put a hand to the side of his head.

"Thought you said it didn't hurt," McCarty said.

"Not on the outside," Zeke said. "But it hurts on the inside. There have been these headaches since the beginning, so bad I nearly go blind, and sometimes I hear things. Voices. Reckon that makes me crazy, don't it, Doc?"

"Hearing voices doesn't necessarily make you crazy," McCarty said. "Unless they're telling you to do crazy things. Do these voices tell you to hurt anyone?"

"No, never."

"I hear voices, the voices of the dead," I said. "Who do you hear?"

"The voice of that Flathead woman the Frenchman left me with," Zeke said. "Her name was Madrigal Yellow Bird and we lived along the Powder River and soon she was in the family way. She died in childbirth during a winter so cold that the trunks of the trees burst, and she took the boy with her."

"What does she say?" I asked.

"She talks about our life along the Powder," he said. "Small things that happened, so long ago now. The morning I finished the cedar shingles on the roof of the cabin. When I played the jaw harp for her. The time she tried to teach me to play the Indian game with the stick and the hoops, and she laughed."

He stopped and wiped a tear away with a rugged hand.

"And she has said nothing about the end of the world?" I asked.

"No," he said.

"Don't you think Madrigal would have mentioned it? Go home to your niece, Zeke. Or turn and steer for the mountains. Find a spot that reminds you of the cabin along the Powder River, and listen to what Madrigal Yellow Bird has to say. But don't expect Judgment Day, at least not yet."

He nodded.

"What's your name?"

"Ophelia," I said.

"May you have shining times, Ophelia."

Then he gently turned the mule in the opposite direction.

"There is one more voice I hear," he said.

"Who does the voice belong to?" I asked.

"The bear, of course."

Then he flicked the reins and urged the mule down the road to the west.

10

The town was a going concern of five thousand residents, and in addition to the Santa Fe depot, there was an associated hotel and dining room, a mill on the Cottonwood River, and a courthouse with a stone barricade around it to make it easier to defend, I was told, in the case of Indian attacks. The barricade had never been used, but the town was ready nonetheless.

We stopped beneath the back porch of the Clifton Hotel, and I asked McCarty how he was feeling.

"Weak," he said.

"What do you think is the trouble?" Delaney asked.

"Something I ate, perhaps."

"Now that you mention it," Calder said, "I'm feeling a bit poorly myself. Headache. Some stomach discomfort."

For Calder to admit he felt at all unwell meant that he felt downright rotten.

"How are you feeling, Ophie?" McCarty asked.

"Normal," I said.

"What did we eat, Jack, that made us sick?" McCarty asked.

"The sandwiches," Calder said.

"What was in those sandwiches?" McCarty asked.

"Just the usual, I suppose," Delaney said. "Ham. Cheese."

"The meat in the sandwiches could have turned," McCarty said.

"Where did they come from?" Calder asked.

"A restaurant along the line," he said. "They shouldn't have been bad. They were kept on the same ice as the general manager's oysters—"

Calder held up his hand.

"Please," he said, fighting a gag reflex. "I don't want to hear about oysters right now."

"Are you two going to be all right?" I asked.

"Of course," McCarty said. "Just a touch of bad food."

"What are your symptoms?"

"Headache, stomachache," he said. "Thirst. Flux."

"Should we summon a doctor?"

"Nothing to be done for a mild case of food poisoning except to allow it to pass," McCarty said. "Let's continue, so we can find something else to occupy our minds."

"No," I said. "Both of you look like walking death."

"You need us," McCarty said. "We'll get a second wind once—"

"Don't argue with me," I said. "We're going to get you a room and allow the both of you to rest for a few hours. I can start my inquiries, and if I find myself in dire need of you, I will send word."

McCarty was too sick to fight, but Calder shook his head.

"I'm fine," he said.

And then he dashed to the edge of the porch and vomited.

"Young Delaney," I said. "Go find Engineer Skeen at whatever roundabout or siding he has placed the *Ginery Twitchell* and tell him about the problem with the sandwiches, and ask if he knows where they came from. Then, personally see to it that the sandwiches are disposed of, so nobody else will fall sick after eating them. I'll take care of getting these two some lodging."

"The hotel is likely full, because of the stranded passengers," he said, while reaching into his pocket and pulling out a card. "But there is a room on the third floor reserved exclusively for railway use. Please hand the clerk this and ask for room 312."

"Thank you," I said.

"Where should I meet you after?"

"Come back to the hotel and check on these two," I said. "If they appear to be recovering, come find me at the station."

He nodded.

Although the Clifton Hotel was a sprawling white clapboard affair, looking something like an overgrown farmhouse, on the inside it was surprisingly civilized. Once I handed the clerk Delaney's card, he rang a bell and a porter appeared to help me get McCarty and Calder upstairs. Calder, of course, refused any help and insisted on climbing the stairs himself.

Room 312 was large, with two good-sized beds, and we placed McCarty on one of them while Calder sat on the other.

"Get in bed," I said.

"Just let me rest for a few minutes," Calder said.

"Shut up and take your gun and your boots off," I said.

He did as instructed, finally, and he stretched out on the bed. He asked me to unbuckle the gun belt and hang it from the bedpost near his head, which I did. Then I took the washbasin down from the chest of drawers and placed it between the beds, so both could reach it and draw it near, if needed. Then I told them both I had better not see them upright until they were feeling better, and after closing the door I tipped the porter a dime for his help.

The hotel was full of passengers and their baggage, many of whom had apparently taken up residence in the entryway just inside the front door, because there were no rooms for them. Some, seeing a new face, asked if I had any news, and I truthfully shook my head.

I left the hotel by the front steps, walked past the two fountains in front, and followed the road—and the parallel railway tracks—to the station. My path was carpeted with freshly fallen leaves, and the low afternoon sun gave everything a golden cast, and I thought it perfect irony that on this beautiful fall day, I was on a desperate case with two sick friends in tow.

The depot was a wooden structure, much like the one at Dodge, except larger. In addition to the main track, there were many sidings, and the looping circular track that went to the hotel. I could see the *Ginery Twitchell* parked safely on the far lobe of this circular track, some hundred yards or so beyond the station; its boiler was apparently shut down, because no smoke came from the stack.

I stepped up on the platform and made my way through the forlorn people scattered about the wooden platform, some with children, who were waiting for some sign the railway would soon resume its scheduled runs. Their hollow eyes avoided mine as I approached, knowing that it was unlikely I had anything of interest to share.

When I tried the knob to the door of the passenger area, I found it locked.

I walked around to the window of the station office and tapped on the glass. The man inside the office was tilted back in his chair with his shoes on the desk, his arms crossed and his eyes closed. I knew he wasn't asleep because his face registered disdain. In the background, I could hear the telegraphic sounder tapping out strings of dits and dahs.

"Pardon me," I called.

"We're closed," he barked, eyes still closed. "That's why the door's locked."

"Please, I am on business."

"Come back when operations resume," he said. "You'll be able to tell when that happens because the sign on the door will read OPEN and there will be these great loud things on the tracks."

"Open your eyes a moment, please," I said.

One eye came open.

I pressed the letter from Strong against the glass.

"This is from your general manager," I said. "It says you are to accommodate any reasonable request I might have, to assist me in my work. My decidedly reasonable desire at this moment is that you open the blasted door so that we may talk without a closed window between us."

The man motioned for me to come around to the employees' door to the office, unlocked it, and held it open while I stepped inside. He was about twenty-five, and his rumpled clothes and red eyes indicated he had not been to bed since the trouble started, and he was drunk with fatigue.

"Sorry, ma'am," he said. "Had I known that you were working for the old man—I mean the general manager—I wouldn't have behaved so brusquely. But you have to understand, ma'am, that since the event, the passengers have been very difficult to control, and several times I feared they would rush the station and occupy the office."

"Don't call me 'ma'am,'" I said. "Miss Wylde, or Professor Wylde, will do."

"Certainly, Professor."

He offered me the swiveling wooden chair he had recently vacated, and he took a stool near the window. The wooden chair was disgustingly warm.

"You're calling it the 'event'?"

I had to admit, it was a better description than *luminiferous aetheric rift.*

"Well, that's just what me and the boys started calling it," he said.

"It'll do," I said, and removed a pencil and my ledger from the satchel. "What's your name?"

"Cecil."

"Last name?"

"Kennedy."

"The wires are still occupied, Cecil?"

"Full of nothing but nonsense," he said. "No blue flame, but maybe we just can't see it in the daylight. I reckon you'll want to know all about when it started. I was sitting here and the first thing I noticed—"

"Not now, but perhaps later," I said. "Tell me about Hopkins."

"Old Hapless?"

"I understand they also called him Lightning."

"That was in the old days," he said. "He got the nickname when he was quite young, long before I knew him. He was one of the first to decipher the code by sound."

"What do you mean?"

"Well, in the old days, from the time Professor Morse received the message 'What hath God wrought?' from the Old Supreme Court Chamber in Washington to Annapolis Junction, in 1844, it was all done by tape. It was a cumbersome thing, having a clockwork device that unwound the paper while a stylus made little pricks in it, which you deciphered by comparing the marks to a code book."

"Where does Hopkins enter this?"

"In 1848, when Hopkins was hired as a messenger for the Morse Company. He went to work at the age of fourteen at the company's office in Frankfort, Kentucky, along with two other boys. Morse was expanding to nearly all points east of the Mississippi, the offices were busy, and juvenile males were so fascinated by the technology that the company could pay them next to nothing. I think they would have worked for free, just to be around the stuff. Well, the other two boys in the Frankfort office were Andrew Carnegie and Jimmie Leonard. You've heard of Carnegie, of course, but Leonard was the real genius. He began deciphering the code coming in by the sounds the relays and the stylus made as it pecked out the messages on the tape. He was the first sound-reader, something the Morse company discouraged, at least until Jimmie Leonard demonstrated that he could reliably sound-read the code faster than the tape could record it. Soon after that, the magnetic relays were affixed to boards, and put in a kind of box—a sounder——to make the clicks and clacks louder, as an aid to copying."

"And Hopkins was one of these early sound-readers?"

"That's how he got the nickname 'Lightning,' because he was so fast at it," Cecil said. "Oh, we still use tape, for the automatic transmission of messages——stock quotes and some telegrams, for example——but the bulk of the traffic on the line is sent by hand and received by ear. No machine can equal the human brain for speed of comprehension."

I doubted that any machine was capable of comprehension, but Cecil seemed comfortable with the idea that machines could think and understand.

"How do you know this history?"

"Every telegrapher knows the story of Jimmie Leonard," Cecil said. "He's one of the heroes of the telegraph. As for Hopkins, well, he told the story often enough around the depot, of having worked with Leonard and Carnegie. We all got tired of hearing it, I'm afraid."

"He would have been how old?" I asked. "In his forties?"

"An old man," Cecil said. "Forty-five. He began losing his hearing a few years ago, but could still copy code by feeling the vibrations of the sounder. Some folks also began calling him 'Hapless' because he was accident prone, always knocking over the inkwell on the desk, or spilling coffee and tripping over things."

"But you didn't engage in such name-calling, did you, Cecil?"

"Oh, no, Professor."

"Of course not."

"Things got right bad at the end," he said. "His sight began failing, and he was often sick. He all right during the day, which is when his shift was, but in the last week or so he was nearly completely blind at night."

"Tell me about his habits," I said.

"His habits, Professor?"

"Yes," I said. "Did he have friends? Where did he live? What did he do in his free time?"

"Not many friends, except for Mackie in Dodge," he said. "That's why Mackie got the camelback key that was Hopkins's personal and favorite. He didn't have any pastimes that I am aware of. Lived by himself in a shack behind the post office. But he liked to eat in the dining room at the Clifton Hotel, and he was especially fond of vinegar pie."

"I can't think of a less appetizing name for a pie."

"Oh, it's not all vinegar," Cecil said. "Some. It's really quite sweet, sort of like a custard. It's not on the regular menu, but one of Harvey's girls would make it up for him special. Sometimes, she would drop it by the depot for him, special. I think she felt sorry for him."

"Is Harvey the cook?"

"No, Fred Harvey is the man that owns the dining hall," he said. "Has one in Topeka, too. Have you ever had the usual food that's found near stations? Awful, ain't it? Well, Harvey has opened up these houses to give passengers—and train crews and railway employees—tasty food at honest prices. He took over the Clifton Hotel last year, and even brought a cook in from Chicago to supervise."

"Were you here when Hopkins died?"

"Yep," he said. "He hit the floor right about where you are sitting. Clutched his chest and keeled over. His heart failed him, is what they said."

"The girl who was kind to Hopkins," I said. "What's her name?"

"Molly," he said. "Molly O'Grady."

"Does she still work there?"

"Oh, sure. And she was plenty heartbroken over the death of the old bird, too. Attended his funeral and cried and everything. The only person there other than railway employees. Helped go through his things."

"When was the funeral?"

"A week ago Sunday, I think," he said. "We buried him in the cemetery, just past the mill."

"So, he was sick and clumsy and going blind," I said. "It appears he wasn't well liked. Did anyone stand to gain anything from his death?"

"He didn't *have* anything, Professor," he said. "You should have seen the inside of his shack. It was just a bunch of rubbish. We just packed everything up into crates and set it outside, to be hauled away. Even the old camelback that he gave Mackie wasn't worth much, as old as it was."

"Did Hopkins have any enemies?" I asked.

"You mean, was he murdered?" Cecil asked. "Yeah, I heard the message on the wire, claiming that old Hapless was murdered. Don't know who was sending that message, but it sounds crazy to me. He was just a sad old man. Other than annoying people with his stories, he didn't hurt anybody."

I closed the ledger and slipped it back into the satchel.

"Oh, one other thing," I said. "Did you notice a strange, dark train pass after the trouble started?"

"Thought I dreamed it," he said. "It was silent and just glided by. Couldn't have been real, I thought. Then I heard some fellows from the maintenance gang talking about it. They swore it was a ghost train, crewed by phantoms. Was it real?"

"Yes," I said. "Thanks. You've been a help."

"Can't imagine how," Cecil said. "The lines are still tied in knots, the trains aren't running, and I'm sort of afraid of the dark. It's not just the lights in the sky, Professor, or the blue lightning on the lines; it's how angry the people are getting about all of this. They seem to blame the railroad."

There was a knock at the window. It was Delaney.

"No relief coming anytime soon?" I asked.

He shook his head.

"Since Hapless died, the railroad has been sending a man from Newton, until someone new can be hired for here," Cecil said. "But with no trains running, I have no help. It's a one-man shop, all day—and all night."

"I will speak to young Delaney here, and see what we can do about that," I said. "In the meantime, use extra caution, and speak to no one about what we have discussed."

I shook Cecil's hand. Then I slipped out, and he locked the door behind me.

"How are things at the infirmary?"

"They are resting comfortably enough now," Delaney said. "They both had a violent fit of vomiting. But McCarty dosed them both with something from his bag, and they quieted."

"Laudanum," I said.

"Did you learn anything of interest here?"

"Perhaps," I said. "Follow me, please. First, we need to see if there is still some rubbish at a shack behind the post office. Then, we need to investigate an angel of mercy and her famous vinegar pie."

"Didn't Grunvand recommend that?"

"Indeed," I said. "But tell me, why wouldn't it be on the menu?"

"Well, that's obvious," he said.

"Not to me," I said. "I don't cook."

"Vinegar pie is good in lean times, because the ingredients can be found in every kitchen, no matter how bare the larder—eggs, water, sugar, and of course vinegar," Delaney said. "It's not something that a hungry traveler would either want or expect at a fine restaurant."

11

From the depot, we walked into town along Fifth Street and then turned east on Main, to the center of town. The post office was in the middle of the block, on the west side of the street, between a general mercantile and a drugstore. We went behind the buildings and found, in the alley, a public well and a cabinet shop, from which there came the sound of wood shaving. Not far behind the cabinet shop was a shack that was about ten by fifteen feet, with one window and a tarpaper roof.

The structure was painted in the same shade of yellow the railways used, and I guessed Hopkins had scavenged drips and drabs of paint that had been left by work crews. Against the wall of the shack were three wooden boxes filled with the personal belongings of the luckless telegrapher, waiting for the rag and bone men.

"Not much of a home," Delaney said.

"Any home is better than none," I said.

"I would have thought he could have afforded better," Delaney said. "We pay our telegraphers a competitive wage, even someone who is old and apparently going blind. Why, this place is a disgrace."

"Is that the measure of a man?" I asked. "What kind of house he lives in? Strange, but I always thought it was what was on the inside that mattered most."

I touched the door of the shack and it opened inward. The inside of the shack was papered with newspapers, and the floor was planked with lumber in different widths and hues. An iron bedstead with a bare spring mattress was beneath the window, and an ancient lamp hung from the ceiling. In the corner was a small stove, with just enough of a top for a rusted can in which to boil coffee. The stovepipe went straight up to the roof, where it disappeared through a hole sealed with tar.

"He must have scavenged all of this."

"Yes, that lamp looks as if it is railway property," Delaney said.

"This was all his," I said. "He made it. It was what he wanted."

"Yes, but what did he do with his money?"

Delaney knelt and started picking through one of the wooden crates. There were bundles of newspapers and books, now swollen and discolored because they had soaked up water. There was a tin can with a label that said PEACHES, but which now held an assortment of pencils. An old gallon coffee can was stuffed with a collection of pipes, with a defect in each, from split stems to burned and cracked bowls. Delaney picked up one of the pipes, a bent briar with a broken bowl.

"Hello there," a man called as he stepped from the door of the cabinet shop. "What are you doing? That's private property."

Delaney dropped the pipe back into the can.

"We thought it was trash," he said.

"Beg your pardon," I told the man, offering my hand as I walked toward him. "We didn't know you were the owner of the structure. We were looking into the effects of Mr. Hopkins, but we should have thought to ask first."

The man, who was dressed in work clothes, was powdered with pine shavings. The little white chips even clung to his beard.

"I own the property," he said, "but I don't own the shack. Nobody owns it, not now."

"Was he your friend?" I asked.

"As much as anyone, I suppose."

The man said his name was Davis and that Hopkins had rented the spot from him for fifty cents a month, and had refused any offers of help to build the modest structure.

"What are you going to do with the shack now?" Delaney asked.

"I suppose I should tear it down for firewood, but somehow I can't stand the thought," Davis said. "I may come around to it, once I get used to the idea of Hopkins being dead and gone."

Dead, I thought, but possibly not gone.

"Can you tell us anything about his personal habits?" I asked.

"He was friendly enough, and would sometimes pass the time with me and the boys in the evening. He was full of stories of his youth, and we never knew whether to believe him or not."

"How so?" I asked.

"He talked about how he learned the telegraphy business as a boy, back in Kentucky where he was born," he said. "He said one of his friends at the telegraph office was Andrew Carnegie, and that was pretty hard to choke down. If he'd been boyhood friends with Carnegie, do you think he would have ended up here? The other thing he claimed was that the inventor of the telegraph had personally taught him the code."

"Samuel Morse?" I asked.

"He didn't say, but that's who we took him to mean. We just listened politely; because he enjoyed our company so much, we didn't want to offend him."

"That was kind of you."

"He was a nice man," Davis said. "Sad, but nice. And gentle."

"I'm sorry I didn't get a chance to meet him."

"You say you're going through his things?" Davis asked. "You can't be family, because Hopkins said he had no family left."

"No, we're not family," I said. "But young Delaney here represents the railroad."

"The girl from the hotel was already here, a couple of days ago," Davis said. "Oh, what's her name? Maggie or something."

"Molly?"

"Yes, the Irish girl with the dark hair and gray eyes," Davis said. "She went through all of the boxes there, and took a look around inside, too. Just like you're doing."

"Did she find anything?"

"Not that I saw," Davis said. "But she didn't know where to look."

"What do you mean?" Delaney asked.

"It was raining the morning she came, and I had the door to the shop open, like it is now, and I was sitting just inside watching," he said. "She went through everything and she seemed to get real flustered about not finding what she was looking for. I had the feeling she was looking for money, so I was not inclined to give her any advice. You're not looking for money, are you?"

"No," I said.

"Then what are you looking for?"

"Clues."

I explained that I was a detective.

"We have fear that Hopkins was murdered," I said. "Do you know anyone who would have wanted to harm him? This girl, perhaps?"

Davis shook his head.

"I just think she was looking through his things, on a kind of treasure hunt," he said. "All those boxes out there, that is trash. It's what the railway fellows came and boxed up after the funeral. But I saved some of the stuff that seemed important to Hopkins."

"Important, how?" I asked.

"The things he used every day," Davis said.

"He kept his correspondence neat, all bundled with string and placed in a cardboard box, for example. His best pipes, some cups, his plates and dishes. I stored them here in the shop, thinking that someday some distant relation might come asking about him."

"Could we see these things?"

We stepped into the shop and Davis brought the box down from a shelf.

"The dishes haven't even been washed," Delaney said.

"He was too sick near the end, before his heart gave out," Davis said.

I removed the cardboard box.

"Have you opened this?"

"I know what's inside, but I didn't undo any of the packets," he said. "It just didn't seem right."

I opened the lid of the cardboard box and thumbed through the correspondence. One packet was from his fraternal lodge, the Order of Railroad Telegraphers. Another bundle was letters from a widowed sister back home in Kentucky, more than ten years of them, and they ended with a letter, dated in 1876, from a physician saying that the sister had died of pneumonia, age fifty-two—and enclosed was a bill for five dollars for services rendered. Another packet was correspondence from an "A.L.V." in Morristown, New Jersey. The latest of these letters, which were all in a precise and competent hand, was January 1859. I attempted to read two of them, but they seemed full of technical jargon and abbreviations I didn't understand.

The last thing in the box was a sheaf of correspondence from the Christian Orphans and Widows Home in Louisville, Kentucky. It took me only a moment to realize what the monthly letters of thanks meant.

"He had no money," I said. "He gave it all away."

"Every penny?" Delaney asked.

"Nearly so, it would seem," I said. "Twenty-five dollars a month to the widows and orphans of Louisville."

"That would leave him very little to live on," Delaney said.

"That explains the shack," I said. "But he was feeding and clothing a dozen widows and orphans a month, according to this letter. I can't imagine that kind of sacrifice."

Davis rubbed his jaw.

"It does put the rest of us to shame," he said. "I'm glad now I made the coffin in which he was buried. Oh, it was from odds and ends here in the shop, but he probably would have wanted it that way. He doesn't even have a headstone up on the hill at Cottonwood Cemetery. There was no money for it."

"I'm sure the Santa Fe will bear the cost of a simple stone," I said.

Delaney was silent.

"Did you hear me?"

"Yes, I'll bring it to the general manager's attention."

"You will do more than that," I said. "It is part of the railway's moral responsibility to its former employee, and you will personally see to it that the stone is erected. You will do that, won't you, young Delaney?"

"Yes," he said.

"I knew you would," I said.

I put the lid back on the cardboard box, and returned the box to the crate.

"Mr. Davis, you have been so kind," I said. "But I have one more favor to ask. Would you mind awfully if we took the box with us? It will be returned when the investigation is over, if you wish."

"Take it," he said. "I have no use for it. If it remains here, it will just make me sad."

I thanked him, and handed the crate to Delaney.

"May I ask your opinion?"

"Of course, Mr. Davis."

"How long do you think I should wait until I tear down the shack?"

"You'll know when it's time."

"But how?"

"You'll find your own cause to give your money and talent to," I said. "It might not be a home for widows and orphans. It could be a hospital, or a public school, or a library. But you will find some civic need that you can fill, and when you do, you won't need the shack as a reminder of sad and kind Hopkins anymore, because the work will be reminder enough."

As we were walking away, with Delaney carrying the crate with both hands, he asked me if I had a charity I gave to, or whether I just gave advice.

"Of course I have a cause," I said.

"What is it, then?"

"If I told you, it wouldn't be a secret," I said. "Now, you go on to the Clifton Hotel with those things, and I'll be along by suppertime."

"A bit hungry, at last?"

"No," I said. "But dining is an excellent excuse for meeting this mysterious Molly with the dark hair, and not arouse her suspicion."

12

It was growing dark now, with flashes of pink and green in the northern sky, so I hurried along Seventh Street toward the Cottonwood River, and the mill. The mill was large, with an impressive dam and associated flumes and traps and races, or whatever they were called, and the mill wheel was turning. Inside, there was the whir of machinery and the slap of leather belts and the low growling sound of the stone. I took the path around the mill and followed the river bank to the north, and on a hill near the bridge where the Santa Fe spanned the river, I found Cottonwood Cemetery.

It was a well-tended cemetery, with an iron fence around it and headstones in neat rows. The gate was unlocked and I slipped inside, looking in the gloom for the grave of the telegraph operator. I found it, tucked into a far corner of the cemetery, a mound of bare earth marked by a narrow bit of wood that had H. HOPKINS lettered in an unsteady hand. There were other wooden markers, white crosses, mostly, representing the uncelebrated dead that kept Hopkins company in the paupers' section.

I sat beside the grave, close enough that I could reach out and touch the mound of dirt. Somewhere along the river valley an owl hooted, and it reminded me of the dream I'd had about the barn owl nest. But the owl that was doing the hooting here wasn't a barn owl, because the call of a barn owl was a blood-chilling screech. This bird, probably a barred owl, was giving the familiar "*Who-Who-Whooo.*"

"Ophelia Wylde," I said.

Now, hidden deep beneath the shadows of the trees in the back of the cemetery, it was full dark. There was not a breath of air stirring, and I could hear some small animals—squirrels, perhaps—rustling in the leaves nearby. I could feel the cold creeping in from the surrounding fields, like a cat bent on mischief, and I shivered.

I rummaged in my satchel, found a taper, and stabbed it in the dirt over the grave. Then I took a match, struck it on the wooden marker, and lit the candle. After contemplating the shimmering flame for a moment—for who can resist staring?—I pressed the match into the damp earth and waited.

Overhead, the northern lights danced.

"Here we are, Lightning," I said. "I know that's what your friends called you, and I hope you don't mind me doing so as well. I received your message, or at least Mackie did and translated it for me, and I would like to help. What can I do?"

I waited for a minute or so, with no reply.

"It's getting a bit chilly out here," I said, "and it is very dark. Would it be possible that you could give me some sign that you're here?"

There was a hollow rap that seemed to come from the air, just above the grave.

"Good," I said. "Lightning, who murdered you?"

A rhythmic burst of raps was the response.

"Slow down, please. Could you give me one tap for yes and two taps for no?"

Another burst of raps, in rapid succession, in similar rhythm.

"I cannot copy the code," I said. "Can you speak to me directly?"

More taps.

It was what I had expected.

In my line of work, I had identified some rules that ghosts seemed to follow, unless they were really elementals or demons in disguise. Unfinished business was at the core of most hauntings, and ghosts often repeatedly delivered a message or performed some action that was associated with that business, but I had yet to encounter any that would answer direct questions. I had hoped the ghost of Hopkins might, considering the unusual conditions created by the rift in the luminiferous aether, be able to converse, but I was disappointed; he, too, appeared stuck in a kind of loop. My guess was that the raps, decoded, would mean, in Morse code, "I am murdered!"

"Thank you for your time," I said, plucking

up the candle. "And my apologies for disturbing you."

I brushed the grass and dirt from my trousers, and by the light of the candle made my way out of the graveyard. Behind me, the owl repeated its lonely call.

13

The dining room at the Clifton Hotel was as bright as the graveyard had been dark. There were candles and kerosene lamps everywhere, and the white linen tablecloths and the polished silverware added to the brilliance.

"I can't remember the last time I was in this fine of a restaurant," I said.

"Well, I know when I was," Calder said. "Never."

He was still pale and shaky, but claimed he was largely recovered from the mystery illness. After I had checked in on him and McCarty in room 312, Calder declared he had spent enough time in bed, and wanted to go downstairs with me. McCarty, however, was still too sick, but said he would try to join us later.

"Think of this as an adventure, Jack," I said, glancing up from my menu. "Here we are, just the two of us, in the kind of place we could only dream about back in Dodge City."

"There's nothing wrong with Beatty and Kelly's."

"Nothing but the clientele, the food, and the service," I said.

Before Calder could respond, a young woman with dark hair and storm gray eyes came to the table and interrupted. She had a white apron over her dark blue dress, just as the other women who worked there wore, and her hair was done up neatly beneath a cap.

"Good evening," she said, speaking mostly to Calder. "Have you been to the Fred Harvey dining room before? No? Then you're in for a treat. We are running out of a few things, because the pantry hasn't been restocked since the trains stopped running, but I'm sure we can find you and your missus something good to eat."

She had a slight Irish accent, and her smile was a bit too broad to be genuine. I wanted to shake her and tell her to speak to me as well as Calder, but I held my tongue for fear of offending her—and I wanted her to be comfortable talking to us.

"We're not married," I said.

"Well, not yet," she said.

I smiled.

"Are you married?" I asked.

"Heavens, no," the girl said, blushing. "Do you think I'd be working here if I were married? Mr. Harvey wouldn't allow it."

"Of course not," I said. "What do you have left that's on the menu?"

"I can tell you what we have left that's not on

the menu," she said. "Vinegar pie. I make it myself, from an old family recipe, and the cook lets me share some now and again with my friends. And I can tell we're going to be friends."

"How?" I asked.

"I just have that feeling," she said. "And I come from a long line of seers. My mother had the second sight, and her mother before her. Yes, I know we're going to be seeing a lot of each other."

"Not if the trains start running again," I said.

"My name's Molly," she said, again speaking to Jack. "Molly O'Grady. What's yours?"

Jack told her his name.

"You must be some kind of lawman, with the great big gun on your belt," she said. "The hotel manager doesn't allow firearms, so you must be some kind of marshal or sheriff."

"Something like that," Calder said.

The girl offered her hand. Jack clasped it, and she stared into his eyes and held his hand just long enough to make me uncomfortable.

"And I'm Ophelia," I said.

She touched my hand, but just for a moment. Her hand was dry and a bit scaly, like the skin of snake. Bu, it just could have been calluses from a life of hard work.

"The vinegar pie does sound good," Calder said. "Save me a slice."

"I already have."

"What do you have left that is *on* the menu?" I asked.

"The roast beef," she said. "That comes locally,

as does the ham. But the oysters are all gone, I'm afraid, and so are the peaches."

I ordered the roast beef and strong tea.

"Very good," the girl said. "I'll make sure you get a special fine cut."

"And for you, sir?"

"Just bring me some coffee," he said. "And the pie."

"Are you sure?" Molly asked. "Our chef, Mr. Robert Phillips, was the head man at the Palmer House in Chicago for years. He does wondrous things with roast beef."

"The Palmer House," I said.

"Oh, yes," she said. "It's famous."

"Yes, I believe I've heard of it."

I made a mental note to avoid meeting the chef. He probably wouldn't recognize me, but there was no reason to risk digging up the past. Chicago, and the Palmer House in particular, were a part of my life that I didn't want to be reminded of.

"Pardon me, sir, but do you have a jacket?" Molly asked.

"I have an overcoat upstairs," Calder said, surprised. He was dressed in one of his many green shirts and a leather vest. "Why do you ask?"

"The dining room has a rule that gentlemen must wear jackets," she said. "But not to worry. We have a supply of jackets we keep on hand for the situation. May I bring you one?"

"If you must," Calder said.

"I would loan him mine," I said, "but I'm afraid it would be a little tight around the shoulders."

Molly nodded and said she would be right back.

"How are you feeling?" I asked.

"About the same as before," Calder said.

"Go back to the room."

"No," he said.

"How can you think of eating pie as sick as you are?"

"Well, it is pie, after all," he said. "Maybe it will help me feel better."

"And maybe monkeys are going to make my bed every morning," I said.

Then she was back, a cheap jacket over her arm. She helped Calder into it, then stepped back and gave him an admiring look.

"Fits like it was made for you," she said.

"It itches," Calder said.

"It's an alpaca jacket," she said. "Mr. Harvey got a deal on them."

Molly left again.

"You could just ask her," Calder said.

"No, I want to watch her a little longer before I start asking her questions about Hopkins," I said. Molly was at the sideboard, preparing our coffee and tea, elbow-to-elbow with a half dozen other girls. "As soon as she figures out our interest in her extends beyond dinner, it will make things much more difficult."

"We don't have a lot of time, Ophelia," Calder said. "You heard her say they were low on food. Things aren't going to get any better until we can find a way to free up the lines."

Then Calder winced and put a hand to his stomach.

"Sure you're okay?"

"Fine," he said.

She came back with the coffee and the tea— and the vinegar pie.

"Molly," I said. "You have such a lovely voice. Did you grow up in Ireland?"

"Faith, no," she said. "I was born in Boston, but my parents were from the home country. They spoke the language, but I picked up very little of it—just the accent. Everybody in my neighborhood back home sounds like this."

"How long have you been out west?"

"Going on three months," she said. "What a change it has been."

I tested the tea, but it was too hot to drink.

"What brought you here?" I asked.

"Opportunity, of course," she said. "I don't have to tell you how tough things have been since the Panic of '73. There just were no jobs in Boston for a hardworking Catholic girl, at least no jobs that a good Catholic would consider. So I came west."

"To grow up with the country," I said.

"Pardon?"

"Just something Horace Greeley said. It's not important."

I thought Calder was going to join the conversation, but he instead concentrated on his pie. He used the side of his fork to separate the tip, then tasted it.

"Delicious," he said.

"Thank you, sir," Molly said. "There's a secret ingredient."

"What is it?" I asked.

"If I told you that, it wouldn't be a secret now, would it?"

Calder took another bite.

"Have you heard any news about how soon the main line would be open again?" Molly asked. "I hope the strike ends soon, because it is putting an awful lot of people in a bad way. I'm all for better wages, and I know the brakemen have an awful hard job to do, but they should think about what is best for everyone."

"Strike?" I asked. "Is that what they're telling you about the shutdown?"

"Why, sure," Molly said. "Mr. Delaney explained it all to us, about how the brakemen had gone on strike again, just like in the spring, and have shut everything down until they get more money. It's awful selfish of them, if you ask me."

"What did Mr. Delaney say about the telegraphers?" I asked.

"That their lodge had decided to go on strike, to support the brakemen," she said.

"And the lights in the sky?"

"He didn't say anything about that," she said. "I know there's an awful lot of wild rumors flying around, about the spirits of the dead talking on the wires, but Mr. Delaney said those were just stories circulated by the brakemen to scare us. I sure enjoy talking to you, miss, but I'd better get back to work or I'm going to be in trouble."

She walked away.

"She doesn't seem like she has the sense that God gave a goose," Calder said.

"I'm not so sure," I said. Then Calder got another one of those pained looks, and put a hand to his side.

"You're making an awful face," I said. "Go upstairs."

"Later."

Ten minutes later, Molly was on her way across the floor with my plate of food, and I had just lifted my cup of tea to take the first sip, when Calder tumbled from the chair onto the floor. I rushed over and knelt beside him, and got him sitting up, but everybody in the room had turned to look.

"Drunk," I heard someone mutter.

"Jack," I said.

"Get me outside," he said. "I need some air."

Molly put the plate of food down on the mess that was now on the table, for Jack had half taken the tablecloth with him when he went down.

"What can I do?"

"Have someone fetch the doctor from room 312," I said. "Hurry."

I got Jack to his feet, and helped him across the dining room, and out the back door. Once outside, he fell to his hands and knees in the grass and vomited violently.

"For Pete's sake," I said, brushing the hair from his damp forehead. "Why couldn't you admit how sick you really are?"

He couldn't answer me because he was retching again.

"Ophie," McCarty called from the doorway.

"Over here," I said.

McCarty shambled over, his medical bag in hand.

"Get me one of those lights from inside," he said. I went back inside, snatched up the nearest kerosene lamp, and returned with it.

McCarty sat down on the grass next to Calder, felt his pulse, and then tilted his head back and peered into the whites of his eyes. I held the lamp so that McCarty could see what he was doing.

"What's your name?"

"You know damn well what my name is."

"All right, what's *my* name?"

"Thomas McCarty," Calder said.

"How are you feeling, Doc?" I asked.

"About like he does, except I've done my purging in the basin in the room."

McCarty rummaged around in his bag, looking at various bottles of pills and liquids.

"What do you think it is?" I asked.

"Food poisoning," McCarty said. "Influenza. Or a hundred other things. I'm sorry I was no help today, Ophie. Have you learned anything so far?"

"Precious little," I said. "There's no sign that Hopkins was murdered. Everyone agrees he'd been sick for a while, with multiple concerns. It was his heart that seems to have killed him, but there were other problems. They said he was even going night blind."

McCarty paused in the search of his medical bag.

"You're quite sure?"

"He was working the day shift because he couldn't see at night any longer," I said. "The man I talked to was quite clear about that."

McCarty closed his bag.

"Is there a pharmacy in town?"

"Yes," I said. "There's a drugstore down by the post office."

Young Delaney came to the door now, alerted by the hotel staff.

"How can I help?" he asked.

"Bring us some water," I said. "And some whiskey."

"Give me your ledger book," McCarty said.

I retrieved a pencil and the ledger from my satchel, and handed it over. McCarty began making a list in his neat, detailed hand. When he was finished, he ripped the page out of the book and handed it to me.

"You go fetch that druggist straightaway," McCarty said. "Give him this list. Here are the things he needs to bring with him. Where's that damn kid?"

Delaney came back with the water and the whiskey.

McCarty gave Calder the bottle of whiskey and told him to take a couple of slugs, for the pain. Then McCarty did the same.

"Now, drink as much water as you can."

"It's going to make things worse," he said. "The vomiting and the flux."

"I know," McCarty said.

"What's wrong?" I asked, suddenly afraid.

"Hopkins *was* murdered," McCarty said. "Night blindness is a classic symptom of white arsenic poisoning. We can perform a field test to prove it, using the things the druggist brings, either on his corpse or if we have some of the dishes he ate from."

"Yes, we have some of his dirty plates."

"Good," McCarty said. "Delaney, did you find out where those sandwiches came from?"

"Yes," he said. "The crew said they came from the kitchen here."

McCarty nodded.

"Is that where Hopkins got his food?" he asked.

"Why, yes," Delaney said.

"Then Calder and I have been poisoned as well," he said. "The murderer is among the staff."

"Molly O'Grady," I said. "The bitch gave Calder vinegar pie."

I pounded my fist into the grass and cursed myself for being so stupid.

"You're both going to recover, right?" I said. "You've asked for something from the druggist to cure you. You didn't eat that much, and surely there's an antidote. The water and whiskey would help, correct? And neither of you are night blind."

"I'm sorry, Ophie," McCarty said, and gave me his kindest and saddest smile. "The water was for our thirst and the whiskey, a general anesthetic. There's no antidote, no cure. Night blindness is a symptom of chronic poisoning, over a number of days or weeks. For a dose large enough to make us this sick this fast, it is surely fatal. White arsenic destroys the liver and other organs, and brings on death by heart failure. Even if we were to survive, we would be seriously impaired, because white arsenic damages the brain and breaks the nerves."

The world spun.

"No," I said. "That can't be right."

"We will have to wait for the tests to confirm it," McCarty said. "But my guess is that they will."

"We've got to stop her," I said.

I reached over and pulled Calder's revolver from his holster.

"No, Ophelia," he said, grasping my wrist.

But I broke free of his grasp and struggled to my feet. My head felt like it was on fire, and my skin as if it were turned inside out. Every atom of my being rebelled against the knowledge that Calder and McCarty were dying. I staggered to the door, with Delaney close behind me. He caught my elbow, but I spun around with Calder's gun in both hands.

"No!" three voices called out.

Delaney dropped to the ground.

"She's got to be stopped," I said, waving the gun.

It seemed an exceptionally heavy gun, and its polished frame and walnut grips felt cold in my hands. I lurched to the dining room, where I spotted her against the far wall, filling a cup from the coffee urn. There was a room full of people between us, and as I brought up the gun, some diners ran while others dove beneath the tables for cover.

"*Putain!*" I shouted. "*Salope!*"

I pulled the trigger, but it wouldn't move. Nothing happened.

Molly laughed.

"So, the famous Ophelia Wylde finally picks up a gun," she mocked, the Irish lilt now gone. "I thought that was one thing you wouldn't do. At least, that's what it says in your books."

"You've poisoned my friends," I said.

"The poison was meant for you," she said, taking off her apron and tossing it to the floor. Then she removed her cap and undid the pins in her hair. She shook her head, and her hair fell to her shoulders.

"Why did you stick around?"

"I wanted to meet you," she said. "And watch your friends die. Um, sweetness, you have to cock the piece before it will fire."

"What?"

"Draw the hammer back."

I looped both thumbs over the knurled part of the hammer and pulled it back until it clicked.

"There you go," she said. "Now you're ready. But don't shoot yet."

"Why the hell not?"

"Because it will be so loud that it will make our ears ring and we won't be able to hear each other talk, of course," she said. "You really are quite bad at all of this, aren't you?"

"Why'd you poison Hopkins?"

Her face was the definition of smug.

"What was it that you searched for in his shack?"

She *tsked!*

"You've had plenty of time, and you're still clueless," she said. "How sad for you. Your involvement was a surprise, but then, it has made things a bit more fun, hasn't it?"

"What's your real name?"

She smiled.

"That, I will tell you," she said, and stepped toward me.

"Stay back," I said, threatening with the gun.

"My name is Moria," she said.

"Who do you work for?"

She smiled.

"I'm the trance medium, psychic mercenary, and ace poisoner for R.J. Benson, the wealthiest New York financier that nobody has ever heard of," she said. "He stays in the shadows, waiting for the right moment, and that moment is now. By this time next week, we'll control everything— the railroads, the telegraphs, the newspapers, the banks. People will submit, because they can't stand the uncertainty of being disconnected from the rest of the world. Once you've had a taste of instantaneous communication, there is no going back to the garden."

"You're quite mad."

That sly smile.

"Oh, but what a magnificently malevolent madness."

"You said it was better that you poisoned my friends," I said. "Why is it better than killing me?"

She smiled, and it was genuine this time.

"Because, dear," she said, coming within ten feet, "just look what I've turned you into."

"What do you mean?"

"I've turned you into *me.*"

I jabbed the gun at her while pulling the trigger, and there was an ear-splitting *bang!* The bullet flew high and wide and lodged into the far ceiling of the dining room, dislodging some plaster. My ears rang and wrists stung from the kick, sort of like after grabbing onto a piece of iron that somebody has whacked at the other end with a hammer. I tried to get my thumbs around the hammer again, to prepare for another shot, but Moria closed the distance between us and grasped the gun over the top with her right hand, pinching the cylinder between her thumb and fingers, preventing the hammer from moving.

"No, not quite like me after all," she shouted, "because I would have put a bullet between my eyes. You seem to be as ineffective at murder as you are at detection."

I thought I heard a train whistle blow.

She wrenched the gun from my grip and tossed it onto the nearest table, where it clattered among the dishes. Then she opened her left hand, revealing a dab of green powder in her palm. She flattened her hand and blew the powder in my face.

I felt dizzy and then went down. I could watch what was happening, but I could barely speak and hardly move.

Moria knelt down and whispered in my ear,

"Not to worry," she said. "You won't die. You'll just be incapacitated for a few hours. There would be no joy in killing you now, because then you wouldn't be able to watch your friends die, knowing all the while that you were to blame. Oh, just think of it—not a thing you can do. Except, perhaps, one thing."

"What?" I croaked.

"Tell me where the key is that Hopkins was using the night he died," she cooed. "An old brass camelback key. Avail Speedwell? It's not at the depot and wasn't in his shack. Tell me, oh just tell me, and I might leave you something in a little vial to save your friends."

"Antidote?"

"Where's that key, Ophelia Wylde?"

She brushed the hair from my forehead.

"Dodge City," I said. "The agency, my desk."

She stood.

"The antidote?" I asked.

"Oh, you poor little idiot," she said. "I lied."

I began to cry.

"How weak," she said. "And how predictable. Now, if you'll excuse me, I have a train to catch."

She walked slowly out of the dining room in the direction of the lobby and the front door. Delaney ran into the lobby, but Moria held up a hand, cautioning him not to move. He glanced at me, and I shook my head.

I heard the door open and shut.

A man in an apron and a tall chef's hat came out of the kitchen and surveyed the wreck of his dining room. Then he saw me, on the floor. He put his hands on his hips and shook his head.

"Ophelia Wylde," he said. "Didn't you cause enough trouble in Chicago?"

"Shut up, Phillips," Delaney said.

The young man knelt beside me.

"Are you all right?" he asked.

"Drugged."

There was the rumble of wheels on the railway track, but not the usual huffing sounds a locomotive makes. It was more of a hum, which increased in volume but deepened in pitch. Then it was gone.

"We've got to go after her," he said.

"No," I said. "Calder and McCarty first."

With difficulty, I told Delaney about the list in my pocket, and told him to take it to the druggist and bring him back. Then I grasped his arm.

"The power doctor," I said. "Doyle Creek. Find her."

Then I lost consciousness.

14

"Am I blind?"

"No," I heard Delaney say. "The lamps are out and the curtains are drawn."

"Why?"

"Because Granny Doom wanted it that way," he said. "How do you feel?"

I sat up in the darkness and heard the bed squeak beneath me.

"My head hurts, like I've had too much to drink," I said. "I had a dream I was flying, that I was an owl searching in the night for something. Is there news?"

"The druggist, Karl Schmidt, came with the requested equipment," Delaney said. "He was familiar with the tests Dr. McCarty had in mind, and he tested the vinegar pie given to Calder, the scraps of food found on the plates in Hopkins's things, and scraps of the sandwiches from the *Ginery Twitchell*."

"What kind of test?"

"Schmidt called it a simplified Marsh test, whatever that is," Delaney said, then he recited what he had learned. "He passed hydrogen sulfide through a solution containing the suspect material, and a yellow precipitate formed, indicating the presence of white arsenic. He said it would not stand up in court, because the yellow precipitate would turn clear in a few hours, but it was enough to confirm McCarty's suspicion."

I knew what the Marsh test was. What detective wouldn't? Before the test was perfected by the chemist James Marsh in 1836, there was no way to prove arsenic poisoning. That's why arsenic has long been called "inheritance powder," because it is odorless and tasteless—and readily available, since it is used to kill rats—and it is easy to slip into the intended victim's food or drink, resulting in symptoms that mimic any number of natural diseases. While arsenic poisoning was still rather easy to commit on the unsuspecting, the Marsh test proved the presence of the poison, and also provided a way of fixing the results, in the form of a silvery-black stain on a piece of ceramic, something jurors could see for themselves.

"There will be time to conduct a proper test later," I said. "What of Granny Doom?"

"The power doctor," Delaney said. "She said the powder that was blown in your face was jimson weed, and that you would fall into an uneasy sleep and have strange dreams. She said you would be on your feet in a few hours, but wanted me to stay with you in case you became frightened."

I heard the scratch of a match, followed by the sizzle and the orange flame. He lifted the globe of a kerosene lamp and lit the wick, adjusted it, and put the globe down.

We were in room 312.

"Where's Calder and McCarty?"

"With Granny Doom," he said. "They're down at the mill."

"The mill?" I asked. "What in the world for?"

"Granny said she needed running water beneath them."

"Why?"

"To keep away witches."

"Me, she means," I said, rising a bit unsteadily. "Well, let's go and show her I'm no witch."

"Are you sure you feel up to it?"

"You can stay here if you want, but I'm going to the mill," I said. I pulled on my coat and shoes, then made my way a bit unsteadily down the stairs, and went out the back door of the hotel. He followed me. The night sky was filled with pink and green tendrils of writhing light. The wind had come up, making the trees sway.

"What time is it?"

"Late," he said. "A few minutes to midnight."

As we neared the mill, I could see lights in the interior. The machinery was silent now, the water diverted from the wheel. Everything was quite still except for the lapping of the river upon the bank, which sounded like someone asking in a low and gentle voice to be freed.

We went through the unlatched door and found Calder and McCarty on the floor, with their shirts undone. They were head to foot within a white circle chalked on the planks, with a flickering candle and a Bible at the center. Just outside the circle was a pan of what looked like milk.

Near the Bible in the circle was an aged woman, gnarled as an oak, with a head of white hair that was pulled back tight and tied with a scrap of leather. Her billowing dress was black, there was a necklace of mussel shells around her neck, and a green sash circled her waist. Her eyes were shut and her paper-thin lips were moving quickly, reciting a barely audible prayer. With both hands, she cupped a lumpy brownish green object, about the size of a walnut.

It was the madstone.

Delaney and I sat down on the floor. The wheels and shafts and belts and other apparatus fixed to the ceiling made it seem, in the flickering light of the candle, as if we were in some kind of cave, with stalactites hanging over us. The sound of the water below was like some subterranean river.

When she had finished her prayer, Granny Doom opened her milky eyes and touched the madstone first to McCarty's bare chest, and then to Calder's. Their eyes were shut and their bodies limp, and they were breathing fast and shallow.

Granny Doom dropped the stone into the pan of milk, where it floated and made a strange hissing sound. I thought that might be a good sign, but the old woman shook her head.

"What's wrong?" I asked.

"It's not enough," she said, in a voice that was surprisingly vigorous. "The stone has been passed down, mother to daughter, in my family since before the time of the Old Pretender. It has absorbed every bitter and vile thing for seven generations, but I am afraid it cannot help your friends."

"Why?" I cried.

"There's too much poison," she said. "And not enough power. The stone can only do so much. They are already on the shore of beyond, waiting to be ferried across the great river to the other side."

"What if we prayed, too?" I asked.

I got on my knees and clasped my hands together.

"*Our Father, who art in heaven*—"

"No, girl," Granny Doom said. "Now, it's not a matter of praying more, or praying harder. I've said every healing prayer I know, and have said them with my heart as well as my lips, and yet the stone still floats. The cost is too high."

"We'll pay you," I said. "Young Delaney here is with the railway, and he can arrange for whatever amount you want. It will be a loan, Delaney. I'll work for the rest of my life to pay if off. Whatever it costs, you must save them."

Granny Doom shook her head.

"You don't understand, lass," she said. "It's not a matter of silver. It never is. Just as the madstones must never be sold, but only passed down, so it is with the healing. You can't pay the price with money."

"Then what?"

"A sacrifice," she said. "Something that is a part of you."

"Yes," I said. "Of course."

This all was familiar to me. A long time ago in New Orleans, when I was young and incautious, I had put my trust in the wrong man and flirted with stealing power, and had nearly been ruined by it. But a price was paid, and I recovered—in time.

"I will give a hand, or a foot," I said.

Granny Doom stared at me.

"An eye," I said. "Both eyes, if that's what it takes."

"You don't get to bargain, as if you were shopping for a Christmas ham," Granny Doom said. Then she laughed, and her laugh was like the rustle of grave clothes. "You agree to pay, or not. Only later do you find out what it was you gave up."

"I don't like this," Delaney said. "It's frightening me."

"That's good," Granny Doom said. "It should scare you, young man."

"The devil often tricks the desperate," I said.

"There are no tricks here," Granny Doom said.

"You won't wake up to find your soul has been taken from you, or that someone else you love had died in their place. It may well be that you will lose a hand or a foot or an eye because of this, or be kicked by a horse or fall sick and become an invalid, but then again it might be something else."

"What else?"

"You might lose something even dearer than your health."

Calder coughed and turned his head.

I scrambled around so that I could pillow his head in my lap, my right hand resting on his cheek. His eyes fluttered open.

Calder blinked.

"I'm sorry," he said.

"What in the world do you have to be sorry for?" I asked.

"For not telling you how I really felt," he said. "I love you."

"Oh, Jack," I said. "I always knew."

He closed his eyes.

"Take care of Doc," he said weakly.

I reached out and touched McCarty's leg with my other hand.

Tears streaked my cheeks like rain on glass.

"All right," I said. "Whatever the cost, I agree. Whatever the price I have to pay, I'll do so gladly. Just so long as they live. So long as they are restored to health. This is all my fault, and I should bear the burden, not them."

Granny Doom thrust the Bible at me.

"Swear on it," she said.

The book was putting off a golden light.

Delaney shrank back into the shadows, terrified.

I reached out my right hand and placed my palm on the leather cover.

"I swear it," I said.

There was a clap like thunder and the candle flame flickered, as if in an unseen breeze. The light from the book rippled and spread like waves over us, just as if someone had dropped a stone in the middle of a pond.

Granny Doom put down the Bible, took up the madstone, and rubbed it in a slow circle against Calder's chest. She did the same thing with McCarty, all the while reciting a verse from the fifth chapter of James, "and the prayer of faith shall save the sick." Then she dropped the madstone back into the pan of milk, where it sank to the bottom, and the milk turned an ugly, dark green.

She picked up the pan and thrust it toward me.

"Drink it," she said.

"What?"

"You must drink it," she said. "All of it."

My stomach turned at the thought, but I took the pan with both hands and brought it to my lips. The smell was indescribable, something that evoked necrosis and putrefaction. I drank two swallows, and then my gag reflex closed my throat, and I put the back of my hand to my lips.

Then I took a breath, closed my eyes, and drank. I kept drinking until I had to tilt my head back to get the last drops, and the madstone clicked against my teeth.

"Good," Granny Doom said, taking the pan from me. "Very good."

I felt like my digestive tract had turned inside out.

"Will it kill me?" I asked, folding my arms across my stomach and gently rocking.

"No," she said, "because you spoke the truth about paying the cost."

"How do you know?" I asked.

"Because if you had been lying," she said, "you'd be dead by now. The feeling will pass," she said. "Everything does, in time."

Then Granny Doom knelt beside McCarty, and tugged open his eyes with her thumb, looking into the pupils. She muttered something to herself, and then scooted around and did the same for Calder.

"Well?" I asked.

"They will live," Granny Doom pronounced.

As if in response, McCarty gave a groan and sat up. Propping himself on an elbow, he looked at his surroundings, and at Granny Doom, and at Calder, stretched inverted beside him.

"What foolishness is this?" he asked.

"The usual kind, Doc," I said. "Get some rest for now, and I'll tell you all about it later."

15

I felt as if I had been trampled into the dirt by a herd of longhorns. My stomach hurt, but it wasn't as bad as before. The fatigue was bone deep, however, and it wasn't just physical, it was spiritual—what kind of fool was I to blithely put my friends in mortal danger? And to allow that girl, Molly cum Moria, to trick me so badly as to sling a heavy revolver around the dining room at the Clifton Hotel and actually fire a shot with murderous intent, albeit terrible aim? It would have been easy to tell myself that my conscience made me miss, that of course I would have never killed another human being, so I really hadn't been overcome by emotion and violated my own principles. That, however, would have been a lie.

But there was much to do. I didn't have the luxury of feeling sorry for myself for very long.

While still cradling Calder's head in my lap, I sent Delaney to tell Engineer Skeen to ready the *Ginery Twitchell* for travel, and then to commandeer any wagon or buggy he could find and bring it back to the mill.

"What's the plan?" Delaney asked.

"We're going after Moria, of course," I said.

"But it's night," he said. "It's too dangerous out on the main line."

"Don't argue," I said. "Just tell Skeen to be ready. And stop by the hotel and have our things, including Calder's gun, which was in the middle of a pile of broken china on a table in the hotel dining room when last I saw it, placed aboard the train."

"Right away," Delaney said.

He still looked pale and shaken.

"One more thing," I said.

"Yes, Ophelia?"

"Stop lying to the hotel staff about the cause of all the trouble," I said. "It might be convenient to blame it on striking brakemen and their telegrapher friends, but in the end somebody might get hurt."

"It seemed the most reasonable thing to say."

I shook my head.

"Just tell them the truth," I said. "It's a mystery that we're trying our best to solve."

Delaney nodded, then left.

Granny Doom began packing her things into a grain sack. She took the madstone out of the empty pan, put the pan in the sack, and slipped the stone into her sash.

"Thank you," I said.

"Do not thank me," she said. "The power came from above."

"When will I know?" I asked. "The price, I mean."

"Not until you know," she said.

Then she paused and regarded me with her ancient, milky eyes.

"Is that what you wanted to hear him say?" she asked.

"Calder? Of course," I said. "Most men have trouble saying what they're feeling. But I don't know what's so hard about it. It's just three words. You'd think you were asking them to confess to a murder."

"It won't change things," Granny Doom said.

"Of course it changes things," I said, a bit shocked and a little offended. "It changes *everything*. It always does."

She shook her head.

"What did you say in response?"

"Well, I said it back."

"No, you didn't," she said. "You said you knew he felt that way, but you didn't return the sentiment. It wasn't equal. You accepted what he had to say, but you kept your feelings locked up tight inside you."

I tried to remember. Had I really not told Calder I loved him?

"Will he stop loving me?" I asked.

"Girl, how should I know?" Granny Doom asked. "He might, but it won't be because of what happened tonight. If his love is real, you can't trade it away for anything."

"And if love is false?"

"Why would anybody want to hold on to that?"

I nodded.

"I don't want to offend you by offering you money," I said, "but I would like to show my gratitude."

"Didn't say I don't take money," Granny Doom said. "What I said is that you can't buy a miracle, just like you can't buy a madstone. For my time, I'll take your money."

I took a ten-dollar note from my vest and handed it to her.

"This is more money than I see in a year," she said. "But considering how you were willing to give away your young friend's railway earlier, I'll take this—and you can consider it a bargain."

"Assuredly."

She tucked the note into her sash, then flung the grain sack over her shoulder.

"This woman you're chasing," she said. "She operates through subterfuge. It is the nature of a poisoner. Take care that you do not assume that to be true which is, in reality, false."

Then she left.

16

It took no more than thirty minutes for Delaney to deliver the message to Skeen, have our things put aboard the express car, and return to the mill with a buckboard driven by a very confused livery owner, a man with a narrow face and a bald head.

"It was not necessary to hire a wagon," Calder said, leaning with his back against the door frame for support. "I can walk to the train."

"Perhaps I'm the one who wanted the ride," I said, climbing up into the seat.

Delaney, who was in the back, reached out a hand and pulled Calder up, and then they both helped McCarty.

"How're you feeling, Doc?"

"Better than I have any right to expect," he said.

The livery owner flicked the reins and the pair of white horses pulled us up Seventh Street. As we rounded the corner at the Clifton Hotel, we could see the downstairs was ablaze with light, and people were standing about at the entrance, with their bags.

"What's going on?" I asked.

"The passengers have given up on the railroad," Delaney said. "They're trying to maintain their place in line for the stage. It's not due until seven o'clock, but the stage only holds six people, and they're afraid to lose their place. By the time the stage actually arrives, I'm afraid there will be fisticuffs."

The buckboard rumbled on, past the depot—where I could see Cecil still barricaded in the station office—and then on down the siding to the *Ginery Twitchell*, which was hissing and ticking as the boiler came up to operating temperature. Skeen was in the cab, twirling valves and reading gauges, and the fireman was stoking the firebox.

He waved at me as we drove past.

"This isn't a horse you can just throw a saddle on," he shouted from the cab window. "But give me another ten minutes, and she'll be ready."

Delaney jumped down.

"I've got to throw the switch to point us west," he said.

The door of the express car was open, and Delaney had stacked some crates on the ground to use as steps. I climbed down from the seat, and Calder and I helped McCarty up into the car.

"What about my fee?" the bald-headed livery driver asked, still in the seat of the buckboard, his foot resting on the brake.

"How much?" I asked.

"Two dollars," he called.

"What a bandit," Calder said. He had found his gun belt in our pile of things, with his enormous gun in the holster, and was buckling it around his waist. Then he removed the gun and flipped the little gate open on the side and turned the cylinder.

"Send a bill," I said.

"In care of whom?"

"William B. Strong," I said. "General Manager, Santa Fe Railway, Topeka."

"That will be another fifty cents, for postage and handling."

"Make it an even three dollars," I said.

He released the brake and the wagon rumbled off.

Calder frowned. He tilted the barrel of the gun up, moved a plunger beside the barrel, and an empty shell casing dropped into his palm.

"There's an empty," he said.

"You don't remember what happened back at the hotel?"

"I remember eating the vinegar pie and getting sicker than a dog," he said. "I went out the back door and threw my guts up in the grass, and then I passed out. When I woke up, we were in the mill house."

"Jack, I have something to tell you."

"Who did I shoot?"

"You didn't shoot anyone," I said. "But while you were unconscious in the grass, I may have borrowed your gun. You tried to stop me, but you were too weak."

"You borrowed my gun."

"Yes."

"Ophelia Wylde reached for a gun."

"Well, yes."

"Were you trying to scare someone?"

"No, I was trying to kill them."

"The girl, Molly O'Grady?"

"Her name's Moria," I said. "Yes, I took a shot at her."

"You missed."

"Badly."

Calder thought for a moment.

"How badly?"

"If I had been throwing a baseball, I would have broken a window."

"This is a four-hundred-and-forty-four-caliber central fire Worcestershire heavy with a thousand grain bullet," he said—or he said something like that, a bunch of numbers and a name which meant nothing to me, and which I can't remember now; and I won't give Calder the satisfaction of reading this before it goes to press so he can correct it. "This gun can do some damage. Was anybody hurt?"

"The only thing hurt was my pride," I said. "And it made my hands and wrists sting."

"You were holding it wrong."

"Could I have that thing, as a reminder?"

"What, the empty casing? Sure."

He dropped it into my hand. I slipped it into the satchel.

"You know," Calder said casually, as he took a cartridge from his gun belt and slid it into the empty chamber, "if your aim had been better, it would have made things much simpler. Want me to teach you how to shoot?"

"Absolutely not," I said. "I am somewhat appalled that you would ask."

He slipped the gun into his holster.

"You're the one who borrowed my revolver," he said.

"You should know me better than that," I said. "You really don't remember much, do you?"

"Nope," he said. "But I remember what I told you in the mill. Do you?"

"Of course."

But I still couldn't bring myself to say it.

"How are you feeling?" I asked instead. "Increasingly better?"

"Surprisingly so," Calder said. "It must not have been a very strong dose of whatever it was that Molly put in the pie."

"Must not have," I said.

Skeen blew the whistle, two short blasts, and we jolted forward.

McCarty, who was on the bench near the post office desk, roused.

"How are you feeling, Doc?" Calder asked.

McCarty breathed deeply, and gave me a look that said he knew more than he was ever going to reveal to anyone.

"Redeemed," he said.

As the train picked up speed, we passed the switch, where Delaney was crouching with the lever in his hand. As soon as the rear wheels of the express car had cleared the switch, Delaney threw the lever back, and then he ran after us. With a surprising burst of speed, he caught up to the open freight door, and thrust out a hand.

Calder caught his hand and pulled him up into the car.

Delaney, panting, fell into a chair.

His hands and face were smudged with grease from the switch, his hair badly needed combing, and his clothes—that fine pale linen suit—was stained with sweat and dirt, and ripped at the knees and one elbow.

"Young Delaney," I said. "I think I like you better this way."

Calder drew the freight door shut, and latched it.

"Calder," I said. "Remember back at the office in Dodge, what Grunvand, the Pinkerton man, said? He said we should try the vinegar pie. How could he know about it if it wasn't on the menu?"

17

There was nothing to do except think, as the *Ginery Twitchell* plunged through the night toward Dodge, and hope that we didn't collide with another train on the way. With Grunvand now suspect, Delaney fretted aloud about the safety of the general manager, and how frustrating it was that communication had been reduced to the speed of a locomotive. McCarty sat in a chair, his eyes closed, arms crossed, dozing. Calder slouched on the bench, his boots crossed, thumbs looped over his belt, and would occasionally glance in my direction—an *accusing* glance, it seemed to me.

I sat at the post office desk, the crate from Hopkins's shack beside me, examining the bundles of letters. I spent half an hour examining the correspondence from the telegraphers' lodge, and another few minutes looking again at the letters from the orphans and widows home. Then I took up the collection from Morristown,

New Jersey, and idly shuffled through them.
Picking one at random, I unfolded it and ad-
mired the penmanship of the author, broadly
spaced letters in bold strokes that suggested an
open, but disciplined, mind. Here and there
were the words *telegraph* and *Morse*. I glanced
down at the signature.

"Alfred Vail, Speedwell Iron Works."

The realization tingled like an electric shock.
AVAIL SPEEDWELL.

The impression on the side of the camelback
key that Hopkins had given Mackie wasn't a
phrase at all, but a name and a place: *A. Vail,
Speedwell Iron Works.*

I went back to the top of the letter.

Morristown, October 14, 1858

Dear Hopkins,

*Thank you for your letter of September 2 instant.
I have enjoyed corresponding with a friend from
the old days at the Morse office, and am glad that
you have made your career in telegraph work.
For me, however, I have left the telegraph to take
care of itself, since it cannot take care of me.*

*My partnership with Professor Morse ended in
April 1848, after I realized that, despite my toil in
perfecting both the device and the code—and the
investment of my family's fortune, and the placing
of Speedwell Iron Works at the disposal of this new
enterprise—I was no richer for it, and in fact had
gone considerably into debt and ruined my health
in the process. I returned to Morristown, and
resumed my old habits, and contented myself with*

knowing that the invention that I was a partner in bringing to the world, has changed that world forever. Such satisfaction must be my reward.

It distresses me to learn how Professor Morse characterizes me as his "assistant" in the great endeavor, although I was the one who grappled with a thousand mechanical details, and also brought the efficiency of the dot and dash system. Morse, like many others, had the protean idea for an electromagnetic telegraph, but he lacked the mechanical knowledge to make the dream real. Had I not stumbled upon his lecture at the University of the City of New York in 1837, become enchanted with the possibilities of the magnificent machine, and persuaded my father and brother to give Morse two thousand dollars and the services of Speedwell Iron Works, we would not be speaking of Morse Code today, but perhaps Henry Code, or any other half-dozen who were on the same trail. But Professor Morse was so endearing, with his charm and his flowing white beard and his story of how, on the voyage back to America from France, aboard the packet Scully, *he envisioned a single-wire telegraph. He was already forty-one years of age then, an artist of some note, a painter of portraits and historical pieces, and he recalled how when told of the passing of his poor wife—while he was away on commission— instantaneous communication would alleviate much human suffering and speed commerce. And yet, this gentle old man who pined after a dead wife, would eventually degrade my contribution to the ages with a single word:* assistant.

No matter.

Those who pursue fame are chasing smoke, and I would rather spend my allotment on earth at work on the real challenges that confront us, instead of constantly improving a self-portrait offered for public adulation. I will not waste my time by challenging Professor Morse, either in court or in the newspapers, and while I hope that my story is someday told—and that day may come when I take up the pen myself—for now, I am content to remain as silent as a picture. I do not seek renown for myself. I care little for the world's applause. But what I do desire is truth as to the history of the development of the electro-magnetic telegraph.

I am grateful, old friend, for your letters.

As a token of our friendship, and the days we shared when the dew of youth was still upon us, I am sending via railway express a package containing the original key that I used at Annapolis Junction in 1844 to receive from Professor Morse, in the old Supreme Court chambers in Washington, the biblical passage he had favored—'What hath God wrought?'—to demonstrate the practicality of our invention. As characteristic of our partnership, I had chosen a different passage, one that I felt more appropriate, but I was overruled and my choice was never sent. It is from Job: 'Canst thou send lightnings, that they may go, and say unto thee, Here we are?'

I trust you will find some use for the old key.

> *Yours most truly,*
> *Alfred Vail*

Sandwiched between two of the letters was a death notice for Alfred Vail from the Morristown newspaper, dated 1859. It listed survivors, but gave no indication of the cause of death.

"Doc," I said, packing the letters back up. "Have you ever heard of a man named Vail who was a partner with Samuel Morse in the invention of the telegraph?"

"No," he said.

"Neither had I, until now," I said. "These letters indicate that the telegraph key sought by our murderous Moria was once owned by this enigmatic Mr. Vail, who died in 1859."

"The same year as the Carrington Event," McCarty said.

"Before his death, Vail made a gift of the key to Hopkins," I said.

"If she wanted the key so badly," Calder said, "why did she have to resort to poison? For enough money, couldn't she simply have bought it from Hopkins?"

"I don't think Hopkins was the kind of man who would have sold it, for any amount," I said. "Or, perhaps the buying or selling of it would have offended the spirit of Vail, and rendered the key useless."

"You think Vail inhabits the key?" McCarty asked.

"Perhaps," I said. "Or it is the focus of his unfinished business here."

I looked out the window, at the dark prairie rushing by and the electric sky above.

"Is Samuel Morse still alive?" I asked.

"No," Delaney said. "He died six years ago, at the age of eighty-one. All railway men know this, for there was a grand celebration in New York a few months before his death, in which he bid the world farewell—by telegraph."

"What time is it?" I asked.

Delaney pulled out his pocket watch.

"A little past five," he said.

"How much longer to Dodge?"

"Another hour," he said.

"You should try to sleep, Ophie," McCarty said.

"Sleep," I said. "Who can sleep when the world is about to be plunged back into the eighteenth century?"

18

Dawn was all broken when we pulled into the station at Dodge, and I was glad to be free of the express car. The stagecoach from Wichita was clattering down Front Street, pausing long enough to throw a bundle of newspapers on the railway platform. I glanced at the *Wichita City Eagle* and its multiple-deck headline in bold type: ASTRAL DISPLAY SPARKS PANIC! TELEGRAPH FAILS, KANSAS BANKS CLOSE, RAILWAY TRAFFIC SUSPENDED.

There was a cluster of people on the platform, both men and women and a few children, and some of them made a rush for the newspapers. Others enviously eyed the *Ginery Twitchell* and asked if rail service had resumed.

"No," Delaney said. "This train is a special."

The crowd muttered its disappointment.

"Check on the general manager," I told Delaney. "Calder, you go with him in case that Grunvand is lurking. Doc, you see if Mackie is about."

McCarty nodded.

"Ophelia," someone called from the crowd. "Ophelia!"

It was Wyatt Earp.

"Somebody broke into your agency," he said.

"Is Eddie all right?"

"The bird?"

"Yes, the raven," I said impatiently, stepping into the street with Wyatt trailing behind me. I could see that the agency was still standing, but the front window—the one that had CALDER & WYLDE on it—was shattered. Somebody, probably Mitford, had nailed a row of boards across the frame to cover the hole. "Did they hurt Eddie?"

"I didn't see the bird."

"Cré nom."

Was this what I had agreed to trade away when I drank the foul brew that Granny Doom had offered? How could I live with myself if something had happened to Eddie?

I rushed across the street and fumbled with the lock on the front door. It was jammed, and would not budge.

"Eddie!" I called. "Can you hear me?"

"Step aside," Wyatt said, and tugged at my elbow. I yielded, and when he had a clear enough space, he lifted his boot and with one great kick broke the latch—and the hinges. The door fell inward with a terrible crash, and I stepped inside, still calling Eddie's name.

There was no answer.

The entire agency had been rifled, and there were papers and books scattered everywhere. The bookshelf had been toppled, and the bust of Lincoln lay shattered on the floor. The newel post at the bottom of the stairs was unoccupied. My desk was on its side, and the bottom drawer was open—and empty.

"I don't know who did it," Wyatt said.

"I do," I said. "They came in a dark train that made no sound."

"The ghost train," Wyatt said, and shivered. "That was about four o'clock, that's what the girls at the China Doll said. I was up at the Union Church, trying to convince the crowd that had gathered there that it wasn't the end of the world. It's not, is it?"

"Not yet," I said, picking through the debris. "And not the world, exactly, but *our* world."

Wyatt shook his head.

"I'm not afraid of much," he said. "I can handle just about anything this town has to offer—Texas cowboys who've had too much to drink and let their guns do the talking, soldiers who'll start a fight just to relieve the boredom of army life, soiled doves who are as quick with a knife as they are with their affections. But this spook stuff—it scares me."

"That's why you've acted so oddly around me?"

He shrugged.

"You're afraid of ghosts."

"Terrified," he said.

I picked up a chair from the floor, turned it upright, and sat down.

"You don't have to fear the dead," I said. "It's the living you have to watch out for. No ghost ever tried to kidnap, stab, shoot, or otherwise kill me. But the list of living human animals who have tried it gets longer all the time."

I sighed.

Then I heard a scratching and pecking sound up above the open doorway. I looked up, and the Ace of Spades moved to one side, and Eddie wiggled through the opening. He gave a hoarse cry, shook his feathers, and then flew down to land on the edge of the upturned desk.

"Eddie," I said. "Oh, poor Eddie. Thank God you're all right."

I reached out my hand. He rubbed his head against my palm, then swiveled his head to look at the mess the intruders had made of the agency.

"Don't worry, we'll find you another Lincoln," I said.

"Nevermore!"

"Yes, we will," I said. "I promise."

Then I asked Wyatt to see if Calder needed any help over at the general manager's car. He should be on the lookout for Grunvand, I said, because he was apparently in cahoots with the ones who murdered Hopkins and wrecked the agency.

"What were they looking for?"

"The spirit telegraph," I said. "The key from the depot, which reminds me. Where's Mackie?"

"Oh, he's all right," Wyatt said. "He got disgusted and locked up the depot and has taken up residence at the Long Branch, where he's been taking turns sleeping and drinking. Strong sent word that he was fired, but Mackie claimed he was too late—he already quit."

"Mackie may be smarter than I've given him credit for."

"You should get some sleep," Wyatt said.

"No time," I said.

"What's so pressing now?"

"I'm going upstairs to fetch some fresh clothes," I said. "And I'm going to take Eddie up there with me, and he can stay in my bedroom, if he wants; I'll make sure he has plenty of food and water. Then I'm coming back down and am going to round up Calder. We're going to climb back aboard the *Ginery Twitchell* and see if we can't catch up with the ghost train. Care to join us?"

"That's the difference between me and Calder," Wyatt said. "He can handle the spooky stuff."

When I came back downstairs, McCarty was sitting in a chair in the middle of the mess, waiting.

"Strong is all right," he said. "Still barking orders from his railway car on the siding, but there's nobody around to follow them. Mackie's drunk, and the telegraphers, Salisbury and Lawson, are down at the newspaper office, trying to help the editors Shinn make sense of the crisis. An extra is planned for this afternoon, and Walter Shinn would like an interview with you, but I told him you were terribly busy."

"Right, Doc," I said. "Thanks. What about Grunvand?"

"Strong said that when the dark train came

through, it slowed enough to allow Grunvand to jump on board. It was obviously planned, he said."

McCarty looked around at the wreck of the office. His eyes were red and puffy, and he was so tired he was shaking.

"Why'd they tear up the office so if they knew the spirit key was in your desk all along?"

"Because they could, I suppose."

"Glad to hear the bird escaped harm," he said.

"As am I."

"So what's the strategy?"

"I have no plan other than chase after Moria and her confederates on the dark train," I said. "I have no indication as to what they may be up to, but the tracks lead in only one direction, so it seems our only choice."

McCarty nodded.

"Skeen is taking on water and fuel," he said. "Should be ready to go in about ten minutes, he says."

"Good," I said.

"I should go pack some clothes as well," he said. "And my Winchester."

"Doc, I think you should stay here."

"But why?"

"You're so tired that you can hardly hold your head upright," I said. "That's one reason. For another, Calder tells me you're not a very good shot with either a rifle or pistol, and I don't want to have to worry about you getting hurt when we finally corner this crew."

"I'm a better shot than you are," McCarty protested.

"Granted," I said. "But you're a healer, not a fighter."

"Then take Earp."

"He's afraid of ghosts."

"So that's his weakness."

"Among others," I said. "Also, there's one more reason I want you to stay here, and it's even more important than the others. If something happens to Calder and me, and God forbid young Delaney, then you are the only witness to the truth. You'll have to tell the Shinn brothers what happened. Can you do that for me?"

"You'll be able to tell your own story," he said. "But yes, I'll do that on your behalf, if necessary. But I want Calder to take my Winchester."

"Thanks, Doc," I said, then took his hand and kissed it. "Get some rest. See you when we get back."

19

Back aboard the express car, I slept.

We raced madly west, in pursuit of the dark train, not knowing if or when we would catch it. Rather than stay awake for every dreary mile west of Dodge—and there were 120 flat and sparsely populated miles to the Colorado state line—I stretched on the bench, pulled a blanket over me, and placed the satchel beneath my head. Before I drifted off, I could hear the pitch of the locomotive increase as Engineer Skeen coaxed every ounce of speed from the *Ginery Twitchell*. I slept surprisingly soundly, considering the events of the previous forty-eight hours— and the risk that, at any moment, we might collide with anything unlucky enough to be on the tracks ahead of us.

Delaney, who had managed a quick bath and a change of clothes (that appeared to be an exact copy of his other clothes) during our brief stop at Dodge, slept as well, on a pile of mail sacks on the floor. I don't think Calder napped for a moment, however, because every time I roused, he was still awake, watching the prairie roll past beyond his window.

We stopped at a way station on the state line, to take on more fuel and water, and I woke. We had, Skeen declared, broken a speed record from Dodge to the Colorado line—two hours and thirteen minutes. One of the Santa Fe employees at the station said the dark train had passed, a locomotive and two cars, only three hours before. We were gaining on them.

"Why didn't you try to stop it?" Delaney demanded of the station hand.

"How were we to know we were supposed to?" the employee, a belligerent young man in denim overalls and a red flannel shirt, shot back. "We have no orders from the dispatcher. The wires are still jacked. And I don't think it was even a real train, because I've never seen one like it. It was all dark, and hardly made a sound."

"The general manager expects us to use our initiative," Delaney said. "You have to consider what's best for the railway, and do your duty accordingly. Next time, I expect more from you."

"You want that ghost train?" the hand asked. "Then go stop it yourself. And while you're at it, you can kiss my caboose good-bye, because I quit. You're crazy, you know that?"

The man in denim and flannel walked off.

"The railway will be docking your pay," Delaney called. "And you should not expect a reference, either."

"My God," Calder said, climbing back aboard

the car. "In five years, this kid is going to end up running the Santa Fe. In ten, he'll probably be running the country."

It was another hundred miles to La Junta, where the old Santa Fe trail crossed the Arkansas River. We had been climbing steadily since leaving Kansas, and were now at four thousand feet of altitude. La Junta—Spanish for "the junction"—was an old town, full of buildings made of adobe. At the station, Skeen again re-provisioned the locomotive and confirmed the dark train had passed. It was only ninety minutes ahead now.

Then we pressed on, another hundred miles to Las Animas on the Purgatoire River—the River of Lost Souls—and more fuel. We were less than an hour behind the dark train, and Skeen said we would catch up with them in the next half hour, because they would be slowed by the increasingly steep grade. The end-of-track, he said, was less than a hundred miles away, on the approach to Raton Pass on the mountainous border with New Mexico Territory.

Twenty minutes outside of Las Animas, while rounding a wide curve, we caught our first glimpse of the train, climbing a grade with the Sangre de Cristo Mountains in the background.

"I reckon I'd better make my way up front," Calder said.

"I'll go with you," Delaney volunteered.

"No, son, you stay back here with Ophelia. How do I get to the cab?"

"There's grab irons on the back of the tender," Delaney said. "Haul yourself up and over, and then you can jump down into the fireman's hole and from there step into the locomotive."

Calder nodded.

"Don't kill anybody you don't have to," I said.

"That still leaves me quite a lot of room to operate," he said.

Then he went forward.

Delaney took the window on one side of the car and I pressed myself against the other, waiting for the next curve so we could see ahead. As we neared the dark train, I could see that it was indeed real, with no skeletons running alongside or phantom crew, but it was strange: there was no smoke coming from the engine, and it had few windows and was smooth, like a bullet.

"I'll bet they're surprised to see us," Delaney said.

A moment later I heard rifle shots, but the track had turned and I was on the wrong side to see anything.

"It's Grunvand," Delaney said. "He has a rifle and is firing back at our cab from the open door of his car. Now Calder is returning fire."

We heard a rapid exchange of shots, then one of Grunvand's bullets pierced the side of the express car and splintered the post office desk.

"Perhaps we should get down," I said.

"Good idea."

We hunched down on the floor near the front of the car, pulled the mail bags around us, and listened to a few more shots. Then the shooting stopped. Several long minutes later, our train began to slow.

"Is it the end-of-track?" I asked.

"I shouldn't think so," Delaney said. "We're still a few miles out."

Delaney went to the window and dared a peek.

"Oh, no," he said.

"What?"

I joined him at the window.

Far ahead, I could see that the last car of the dark train had separated from the rest. It was now rolling down the grade, toward us.

"This ought to be interesting," Delaney said.

We could feel our train hesitate as Skeen considered his options. Then the floor beneath us jolted forward. Our engineer had apparently decided the best way to deal with the runaway car was to meet it full speed.

"Your idea of interesting is nothing less than terrifying," I said.

"Brace yourself," he warned.

I barely had time to grasp a handhold before there was a deafening sound and the floor of the express car buckled. The impact knocked both of us to the ground. Pieces of the dark car went flying past our windows, and we could hear and feel some pieces being ground up and spit out beneath the drive wheels of the *Ginery Twitchell.*

"Are you hurt?" Delaney asked.

"No," I said. "And we survived."

"But we are not unscathed," Delaney said, helping me to my feet. "That sound you hear coming from the locomotive is the loss of steam. The boiler is intact—or we would have been blown to a thousand bits—but a steam line must have been damaged."

Calder came through the door, rifle in hand.

"You're both standing," he said. "That's good. Skeen wants you up front."

"Why?" I asked.

"He wants to unhook the express car so we can make it over this next hump," he said. "The end-of-track is only a couple of miles away, but Skeen doesn't think we can make it by pulling the car. Can you do that, Delaney?"

"Of course," he said.

"What will happen to the car?" I asked.

"It will roll backward until it goes off the tracks on a curve," Delaney said. "Then it will plummet down the side of the mountain."

"Can't you set the brake?"

"No brake on Earth will hold it on this grade," he said.

"But it's carrying United States mail," I protested.

"If we don't let it go," Calder said, "Skeen is afraid we won't make the hump. If we don't make the hump, the car will drag us back down, and it will be us going over the side of the mountain as well."

"Well, people can write more letters," I said. "Let's go."

I followed Calder between the cars, with the road rushing beneath and the wind buffeting us.

"Don't look down," he shouted.

"Yeah, I remember from before," I said, then

grabbed one of the irons and started hauling myself up onto the top of the tender.

"What, before?" he asked, confused.

"Never mind," I said, balancing myself on the water tank. "That was a dream."

Then there was a lurch as Delany pulled the pin on the express car. I lost my balance, and Calder caught me with his free hand before I fell. His arm was amazingly strong, and his chest felt like a slab of wood. I kissed him before he could object.

"Dammit, Ophelia, quit fooling around."

"Who says I'm fooling?" I asked. "We might not get another chance."

Then he released me and I inched myself forward, around the piles of wood, and climbed down to the front of the tender, where I could see into the cab. There were bullet holes in the front panels, a corner had been knocked away, and near the front of the engine I could see steam bleeding from a ruptured pipe about the size of my wrist. Both Skeen and the fireman were engaged in what appeared to be serious and desperate mechanical work.

Calder jumped down next to me.

It was cold, and I buttoned my coat and turned up my collar.

"Where's Delaney?" I asked.

"I don't know," Calder said.

"He made it off the express car, right?"

"I'm here," Delaney said, scrambling down.

"You've ruined your clothes again," I said.

"I had to go down between the cars," he said.

"I couldn't reach the pin from either side. I barely managed to make it back up on the tender."

The *Ginery Twitchell* was slowing at an appreciable rate now, and making some disturbing grating and ringing sounds. By the time we made it over the next crest, we were only going as fast as a person could run.

"How far until the end-of-track?" I asked.

"You can see it," Delaney said. "A quarter of a mile."

The dark train had stopped ahead of us, near the end of the tracks, amid a cluttered work area. There were pyramids of railway ties and stacks of rails, tools and telegraph poles, and spools of wire, and a cluster of white tents beyond.

"Where is everybody?" I asked.

"Waiting for the tunnel on the New Mexico side," Delaney said. "You can see the start of it, over on the cliff face. Until the tunnel is finished, nothing else can happen. And winter is nearly upon us, and work is slow at this altitude. It's late. They may have knocked off for the day and gone into town."

"What town?" I asked.

"Trading post, really," Delaney said. "This used to be the old trail over the mountains. There's a cluster of buildings, including a stage stop, just over that ridge."

"How high are we?" Calder asked.

"Nearly eight thousand feet," Delaney said.

"Bring us to within a couple of hundred yards," Calder told Skeen. "Then shut it down."

"That's about as far as we can go, anyway," Skeen said.

"What do you think they're doing, Ophelia?" Calder asked.

"I reckon they're waiting to see what we do."

We had been chasing the dark train all day, and now it was late in the afternoon. There was another hour or so before sunset, but the sky was already gloomy, with banks of rolling clouds lit up from behind by the pink and green flashes of the northern lights.

"Jack," I said. "What do we do?"

He looked at the sky.

"Wait," he said.

In ten minutes, it began to snow. The flakes came down big and wet and limited our vision to about twenty feet in any direction. Calder said that's what he had been waiting for, and he gave the Winchester to Delaney.

"Know how to work that?"

"Sure," Delaney said.

"Good lad," Calder said. "Mr. Skeen, what about you?"

Skeen smiled, then slumped heavily on the floor of the cab. Blood covered the front of his bib overalls, and he held one arm close to him, like a bird would with a crippled wing.

"I would love to oblige you, but it seems I'm otherwise indisposed," he said. "And my union might have something to say about this kind of work not being part of my official job duties."

"And getting shot is?" I asked, taking his hand in mine.

Calder knelt down and undid one strap of the overalls. Then he pulled the denim out and took a look.

"It's passed through your shoulder," he said. "Looks like it busted your collarbone. I know it hurts like hell, but you'll live if you don't bleed to death."

"Calder," I scolded.

"We'll get it packed with rags," Calder said. "So you don't bleed. At least not to death."

The fireman volunteered to stay with Skeen. He seemed relieved to have an excuse to stay in the cab.

Calder nodded.

"All right," he said. "We have to move now. Ophelia, if you think things are going bad, get yourself to that trading post and catch the first coach out of here."

"If things go bad, I'll know it," I said. "I'm going with you."

"Don't be foolish."

"Just shut up. You're not going to win this fight," I said.

Calder cursed.

"All right, but stay behind us. Do you understand?"

We crept forward, yard by yard down the track, the snow sticking to our hair and stinging our eyes. There wasn't much on the ground yet, so at least we didn't have to wade through it. After what seemed like an eternity of feeling our way through the storm, Calder held out his hand, indicating that we should slow down.

"All right," Calder said. "Delaney, I want you to go quiet as you can to the front of that car, then wait. I'm going to come in through the back of it. Once you hear me inside, then make your move. They'll be expecting me, but not you. If we're lucky, Grunvand is the only one who's armed."

"What do I do?" Delaney asked. "Once I'm inside?"

"If Grunvand is still standing," Calder said, "then you shoot him. Don't hesitate. He's already wounded Skeen and tried to kill the rest of us by rolling a train car at us, so there's no point in trying to take him in one piece."

Calder turned to me.

"You stay here," he said, "right here. Don't move from this spot."

"But Jack—"

"No," he said. "Visibility is poor and I need to know exactly where you and Delaney will be. Don't walk into the middle of this, because I don't want to shoot you by mistake."

"I understand," I said.

Then Calder tapped Delaney on the shoulder, and they disappeared into the snow.

20

I've never considered myself a patient person,
and standing in a snowstorm by an incomplete
railway track on the side of a mountain pass,
while waiting for my partner and a young friend
to ambush a gang of murderers, did nothing to
disprove this assessment. Every minute was a
fresh hell of anxiety, near panic, and feared
mental collapse.

Then came the expected gunshots.

I had expected them to be louder, but they
were strangely muffled by the snow. I counted
three shots, and then silence. I waited until I
could bear it no more, and then I called out.

"Jack."

No response.

"Jack!"

I ran forward, and I could see the vestibule
door of the car was open. There was a figure
standing in the vestibule, back to me. As I drew
closer, I saw the man's head, and the monkish

hair, and knew it wasn't Jack. My heart sank, because I realized it was Grunvand.

"Oh, Jack."

Grunvand turned then, a stiff sort of turn. Both of his hands were clutching his chest, and even through the snow I could see the blood that poured through his fingers. He looked at me with wide, pleading eyes, then pitched sideways and fell beside the tracks.

I ran up the vestibule steps and into the car.

Jack was kneeling beside Delaney, who was on the floor next to the Winchester. He was holding his side.

"Oh, no," I said.

"He hesitated," Jack said. "Why did you hesitate?"

"At the last moment I thought it possible to take him alive," Delaney said. "I thought he represented a valuable intelligence asset the railway could make use of. You had the drop on him, as they say, and it seemed he was about to surrender his gun to me."

"It was the road agent spin," Jack said. "Oldest trick in the book. I've used it a few times myself."

Jack pulled Delaney's hand away, pulled back his coat, and examined the hole in his cream-colored vest.

"I'll be damned," Jack said.

He pulled out Delaney's pocket watch. The crystal was shattered and the lid was punctured, but the lead slug was flattened in the guts of the watch.

"Talk about stopping time," Calder said,

pulling Delaney to his feet. "You're going to have a nasty bruise, and maybe a broken rib, but you'll be all right."

Delaney made a face that said yes, a rib was cracked, if not broken. Calder ejected two shells from his revolver and replaced them with cartridges from his belt. He did not put the gun back in its holster, but held it at the ready.

The interior of the car was richly appointed, with lamps and couches, tables and chairs, and a bed, but otherwise empty.

"Where are the others?" I asked.

"They must have heard us by now," Jack said, picking up the Winchester and handing it to Delaney. "We are at a disadvantage here, so I say we press on."

Then Calder walked to the front of the car, went through the door, and tried the knob to the next car, the one just behind the locomotive. It was locked. He cocked the revolver, then drew his leg back and kicked the door in.

The interior of the car was filled with a blue mist.

Calder followed the barrel of his gun inside, and Delaney was close behind.

"What in the world?" Jack asked.

In the center of the car, which was as richly appointed as the other, was a small circular table, and in the middle of the table was the spirit key. On one side sat Moria, and on the other was a finely dressed gentleman of fifty-five or sixty years, with black hair that had gone to gray at the temples. Their hands were clasped tightly together. Moria's eyes were rolled back in her head so that only the whites showed.

"It's a séance," I said quietly.

"Don't shoot," the man whispered, his eyes darting over at us. "I'm afraid to let go."

"Put down your guns," I said, stepping forward.

Jack put a hand on my arm.

"No, it's all right," I whispered. "She's not seeing anything right now, not in this world, and we know where their hands are."

"How many more on the train?" Calder asked. "Engineer? Fireman?"

"No more," the man said. "It's just us."

Delaney shook his head.

"Can't be," he said.

"Stay here," Calder said. "I'll go check."

I took a seat away from the table, and I motioned for Delaney to do the same.

"You must be Benson," I said.

"How do you know me?"

"Moria told me," I said. "After poisoning my friends."

"Have you made contact with Vail?" I asked.

Benson looked surprised. His eyes had a strange, unfocused quality.

"Figured that one out on my own," I said. "AVAIL SPEEDWELL. I should have had it from the start. But it took finding the letters from Hopkins's shack before I put it together."

"Please," Benson said. "Be still. We are at grave risk."

"No, I don't think I will be quiet," I said. "You and your partner have caused me, and the rest of the country, too much trouble. Tell me why the key is so important, and why you had to come here."

"Closer to the sky," Benson whispered. "At the end of an unfinished line."

"Like an incomplete message."

"Yes," he said.

"Why? What do you hope to gain, other than sending us technologically back to our antebellum past? It has to do with incomplete messages, doesn't it?"

"The future is just another kind of incomplete message," he said. "A signal that has not been received yet. For someone to be able to decode the future, there would be no limit to the possibilities."

"This is what Moria sold you."

"I met her a year ago, while seeking a surer way to profit in the stock market," he said. "She did some trance readings for me that proved amazingly accurate, but not repeatable. It was a random sort of thing. Then, in a trance, during a time of a ripple in the luminiferous aether, Moria made chance contact with the spirit of Vail—and received convincing intelligence from the future."

"What intelligence?"

"This train is the result," he said. "It runs on electricity."

"Impossible," Delaney said.

"It's true," Calder said, coming back into the car. "There's nothing in the inside of the locomotive except bundles of wires and strange-looking devices of shining metal. No engineer, no fireman. Whatever is making this thing run ain't steam."

"Wasn't this machine enough?" I asked. "It's worth unimaginable fortunes."

"Nothing is ever enough," Benson said. "Moria swore that if we waited until there was a tear in the aether, we could establish permanent contact with Vail. She said she had a way of keeping him here, that we could have all of the information about the future we wanted, just like a stock ticker."

The key crackled and glowed brightly blue. Moria began muttering something about patents and contracts and government grants. Then she began giving the results of the Whig National Convention in 1844, the one held in Baltimore.

"Henry Clay," she said. "Henry Clay, nominated for president."

Benson cocked his head to one side, listening.

"You're night blind, aren't you?" I asked.

Benson's lips trembled.

"Do you know what she's done to you?" I asked. "She has poisoned you. Night blindness is a symptom of white arsenic poisoning, administered over a period of time. Tell me, was it in the vinegar pie?"

"Oh, God."

"At least she's consistent," I said.

"It was the only thing she knew how to cook."

"It wasn't bad," Calder said. "Deadly, but tasty."

"Please, you have to help me," Benson said. "A doctor. Find me a doctor."

"It will do no good," I said. "There's no cure, no antidote. By the time you are night blind, death is certain. Your heart will fail, most likely."

"Professor Morse," Moria asked, her voice deep, her chin up. "Professor Morse, is that you? I think I've found the solution to the cypher. Yes, dots and dashes. No, wait. Another message coming now. Great loss of life, a ship at sea. It is April 14, Professor."

"We shouldn't be listening to this," I told Calder. "Shut her up."

"Gladly," he said. He removed his kerchief, rolled it up, and gagged her by tying it around her face. Her eyelids trembled, but she remained in the trance.

"Tell me how Moria planned on trapping Vail."

"We needed the key first," Benson said. "She determined it was the only thing that Vail would directly interact with. And then the magnetic coils from the engine. The lines which run from the key are tapped directly into them."

"So you were going to suck him out of the spirit world and put him in a bottle?" Calder asked.

"Something like that, yes."

"Ain't going to happen," Calder said, and before I could stop him, he jerked the wires out of the back of the key. The blue mist in the car grew denser and began to pulse, and we could hear a curious hum coming from the electro-magnetic locomotive.

"You've killed us," Benson said. "If the wires are disconnected, the infernal machine will destroy itself."

"How much time do we have?"

"Three minutes," he said. "Perhaps less."

"Alfred Vail," I said aloud. "Time is short and you must listen to me. You think you're alive, but you're not. You've been dead for some years, and have been trapped in the aether. Do you hear me, sir?"

The key on the table clicked several times.

"I know a little code," Delaney said. "That means yes."

"Shouldn't we leave now?" Calder asked.

I shushed him.

"Your unfinished business has now drawn to a close," I said. "You will receive the recognition you deserve. People who care about such things will know. Starting tonight."

More clicks from the key.

"Good," Delaney translated.

"But there is one thing we require," I said. "The network that you created must be healed. Can you seal the rift, close the door between the living and the dead, and quiet the lines?"

Silence.

"You were a good and humble man in life," I said. "You avoided conflict and strife, made peace where you could, and used your gifts for the good of all humanity. I ask nothing more of you now."

The key chirped.

"Done," Delaney said.

"All right," I said. "Let's go."

Calder hauled Moria up, and Delaney pried her hands away from Benson's. I hesitated for a moment, and then grabbed the spirit key and threw it into my satchel.

"Come on," Calder told Benson. "Let's go."

Benson shrank from him.

"No," he said. "It is no use. I am already dead."

I grabbed his collar, but Delaney pulled me away.

"We have to go," he said.

Moria could not, or would not walk, so Calder carried her in his arms. We ran out of the car, stumbling down the steps to the road bed, and then running through the snowstorm back toward the *Ginery Twitchell*. Behind us, the bullet-shaped train was glowing an intense shade of blue, so much so that it cast our shadows before us.

Delaney paused, holding his ribs, and tried to look back.

"No," I said. "Keep going. Don't look back."

He turned and I slipped my arm through his to keep him in the right direction.

Then there was an indescribable sound, like that of a hundred thousand bees, and the glow behind us became brighter than daylight. I could feel the heat from it on the back of my neck. Then there was an explosion that made the air ripple and the wave knocked us facedown in the snow.

I must have lost consciousness, for the next thing I remember was Calder pulling me to my feet. The storm had passed and the night was completely dark, with untold millions of glittering stars in the sky above us, with just a few wispy clouds.

There wasn't a trace of anything in the sky that didn't belong.

"It's over," he said.

"The dark train?" I asked.

"Not a trace of it," he said. "Nothing."

"We'll let people think of it as a ghost train," I said. "It will be easier that way. Where's Moria?"

"I've got the handcuffs on her," Calder said. "And the kid is guarding her. We'll take her back to Marion County to stand trial for the murder of Hopkins. I don't think we can make any charges from what happened here stick."

"No," I said. "I suppose not."

"Come on," Calder said. "You're freezing. Let's find that trading post and get warm. I'm sure the railway will send someone looking for us by morning, because I'll bet the lines are already open."

"And I would bet you're right," I said.

Calder nodded, then rubbed the back of his right ear.

"There's just one thing I don't understand, Ophelia. Why did you grab the spirit key before we got out of the train? Hasn't it caused enough trouble? I mean, shouldn't it have been sucked back to wherever the train went?"

"That's the thought that crossed my mind first," I said. "But then I realized it wasn't part of that world, it's part of ours. The key should be in a museum, and I'm going to keep it until the day it is. AVAIL SPEEDWELL. It sums up Alfred's legacy quite well, I think—and a promise is a promise."

"But what if it's still, you know . . ."

"Haunted?"

He avoided my eyes.

"Oh, Jack," I said. "Don't be such a fraidy cat. You're starting to sound like Wyatt Earp."

21

One morning on the last day of October, after leaving Calder sleeping, I descended the stairs from the rented room to the agency, where I busied myself with making tea. I stoked the belly of the cast-iron stove with a few logs, put the kettle on top to boil, and closed the black door and brushed the ashes from my hands.

It was chilly downstairs, and I pulled my robe tight around me and considered what to have for breakfast. Did I want ham with my eggs, or bacon? Then I laughed out loud, because I realized that ham or bacon was the heaviest choice I had to make. My mind was free and my heart was light. The case of the spirit telegraph was now closed, the world had returned to what passes for normal, poisoner Moria was in jail in Marion County and was certain to be convicted, based on the results of the Marsh test, and my personal life was blessedly free of anguish.

It felt so odd to laugh that I self-consciously apologized to Eddie, who was watching unhappily from the bust of Jefferson above the bookcase. I knew he was unhappy because he was stretching his wings in an odd, diagonal manner, and one of his claws was raking the president's plaster hair.

"I know it's not the same," I said. "But you'll just have to make do until we can find one of Mr. Lincoln. Honestly, I don't know why it would make any difference. It seems to me one dead president's head would be just as good to sit on as another. But no, you must have the Great Emancipator."

Eddie regarded me with a critical eye, but said nothing in return.

Then there was a knock on the door and the expressman left a package tipped against the front door. Thinking it might be some corre-spondence or even a remittance from my editor, Garrick Sloane of Boston, I retrieved the pack-age and locked the door behind me. Then I sat at my desk and tore open the brown paper wrap-ping, and lifted the lid of the box inside.

I gasped.

Nestled inside a mound of cotton was a small brass cylinder, green with age, attached to a skele-tal bird's foot.

There was also a letter inside the box.

Ellwood Manor, Virginia
October 14, 1878

Dear Miss Wylde,
  Forgive the intrusion, but I believe it appropriate that you have the enclosed. As you will see, it is

clearly meant for you. The story of how I came to find it is most surprising, because I awoke from a dream in the small hours before dawn this morning, a dream in which I was searching an owl's nest in an old barn on a corner of our property. Ordinarily, I refrain from such explorations, considering the history of the land here, but something about the dream convinced me that I must immediately go to the barn and search. I did, and, in a swale, found a barn owl's nest, just as it was in my dream, and in the nest, among the bits and bones and debris from decades past, found the enclosed. Having read your books, and knowing your biography, I knew immediately that the message inside was meant for you, and I also knew where in Kansas to direct this package. Allow me to give you some history that may help you understand the context of the message.

Ellwood Manor, you see, was used as a field hospital during the Battle of the Wilderness in May 1864, just a few days after the Battle of Spotsylvania Court House—the battle in which you believe your dear husband, Jonathan, was killed. The home, which was owned by the secessionist Lacy family, was first used as a field hospital by the rebels, then commandeered by the north. My parents, who were the caretakers of the home, had sent me to live with an aunt by the time of the battle. General Grant made his field headquarters nearby, and in the wake of the slaughter the house became a morgue, and the yard, a cemetery.

Afterward, my parents were sent to the Old

Capitol Prison in Washington for the duration of the war. Ellwood Manor was vacant for more than eight years, during which time it fell into disrepair, a home fit only for ghosts and squatters. Recently, however, wishing to reclaim my birthright, I have returned to Ellwood Manor, and live in the caretaker's home with my husband and our daughter, where we have managed to make a life where once there was so much death. Had I returned sooner, however, your message probably would have been delivered earlier.

Strangely enough, my husband, too, is a veteran of the battles here, and we met five years ago, on my first visit back to the estate since my childhood, when he was taking a measure of the once bloody ground. He is away for the week on business, but I am anxious to share the discovery with him, although he is reticent to talk about his experiences during the war, and has a limp as a constant reminder of those bad old times.

As to the unusual method of communication employed, I can only guess that the remains must belong to one of the pigeons infrequently used to relay messages back to the telegraph posts, either by the army or the newspaper correspondents. Perhaps your Jonathan, or someone on his behalf, managed through an especially eloquent plea, or a well-placed bribe, to have your message sent as well. The unlucky bird must have fallen prey to a barn owl, a bad stroke of luck that resulted in the communication being undelivered these fourteen years.

If not for a dream, it would remain undelivered still.

*Do not hesitate to call upon me, if I could be of
any further service; though our distance is great,
I feel we share a special kinship. Until then, I
remain your trusted but distant friend.*
          Very truly yours,
          Mrs. Jas. (Catherine Ann) Carter

My hands were shaking as I put down the
letter. I picked up the pigeon foot, with the attached brass cylinder, and removed the corroded
green cap. Inside was a tightly rolled message.

I teased the brittle paper out of the tube with
my fingernails, then carefully unrolled it. At that
moment, the teakettle began screaming, adding
to the sensation that my nerves had suddenly mi-
grated to the outside of my body. But I could not
tend to it until I read the message:

MRS. J WYLDE, WOLF RIVER, MISS
HUSBAND BADLY WOUNDED
SPOTSYLVANIA MAY 13 BUT NOW
RECOVERING FIELD HOSPITAL
EXPECTED TO LIVE SENDS LOVE.

Mechanically, I went to the stove. I flipped up
the whistle to silence it, then removed it from
the heat. I walked back to the desk, sat down,
and read the message once more, and then a
dozen times after that. Why, if Jonathan had been
expected to survive, had someone been buried
under his name there? And what of the blood-
stained book of Whitman—*Song of Myself*—that
he had carried into battle and that had been

returned to me? Had he taken an unexpected turn and died before being able to return home? There were no clues to these mysteries in any of the 115 characters of the message.

For thirteen years, I held trance séances in which I tried to contact his spirit, awaiting the coded message that he had proposed beforehand, which would prove that our love had survived death. It never came.

There was a rattle on the stairs behind me, and Calder descended.

"I heard the kettle," he said, buttoning his vest.

"Yes," I said absently. "Sorry to disturb you."

"Time I was up, anyway," he said. "I have papers to serve and then there's the matter of Neal Jones, who appears to have skipped on his bond for theft. I may have to make a trip to his dugout in Comanche County to bring him back."

I packed the skeletal claw and the other things back in the box, and slipped it into the top drawer of my desk. Calder came over and kissed me on the top of the head.

"Sounds like a busy day."

"Yes, but I have time for breakfast over at Beatty and Kelly's, if we hurry," he said. "What do you fancy this morning with our eggs—ham or bacon?"

"Jack," I said. "After I finish writing my account of the case of the spirit telegraph, which will take a month or two, I may want to make use of that lifetime railway pass I've earned and go east for a week or two. Take the manuscript in person to my publisher, Mr. Garrick Sloane in Boston. I would like to meet him in person. Would you mind?"

"No, of course not," he said. "There's plenty here to keep me busy. Unless you'd like some company."

"I was also thinking of visiting the Spotsylvania Court House and seeing where the battle was," I said slowly. "I've never been there, and I think perhaps this is a trip I should make alone."

Calder nodded.

"Are you going to try to find Jonathan's grave?"

"Perhaps," I said. "No, that's a lie. Yes, that's exactly it."

Calder thought for moment while he pretended to fix his cuffs.

"Why now?" he asked. "Has something changed?"

I said I didn't know.

"Will you tell me when you do know?"

"Yes," I said. "Certainly."

"Well, time is wasting," he said. "I should be on my way. Join me for breakfast, if you have a mind. Or not."

Things weren't as simple as ham or bacon any longer.

22

The days passed and winter came. The time was like a waking dream, going every day to my desk downstairs, writing all day, feeling the distance grow between Calder and me, but not knowing what to do about it. Then one day the account was finished and I packed it into a box and bound it with string and boarded the east-bound Santa Fe at the depot.

In less than a week, I was in Virginia.

It was the middle of December.

The trees were skeletal and the sky was pewter. It was cold, not as bone-chillingly cold as the Kansas prairie, but a routine kind of cold that left one numb, with blue lips and clumsy fingers. I had stepped from a coach on the Orange Turnpike to the lane leading up to Ellwood Manor. It was a walk of less than a half mile, and the red two-and-one-half-story manor house with its white portico was easy to spot. This was not my destination, however, and I continued on to one of the many dependent structures, a modest house that was near an orchard.

As I approached, I could see a little blond-haired girl of five or six, swinging on a rope that hung from the branch of a heavy oak. She was bundled in a heavy coat, a scarf and mittens, but her hair followed her parabola like the tail of a golden comet. A woman about my age stood nearby, occasionally giving the girl a good shove, and laughing.

They were sixty yards away. As soon as I stepped up the walk, they were cut off from my view by a corner of the cabin. Knowing it must be Catherine Ann Carter and her daughter, I considered going directly to them, but my hands were cold. Also, I decided it might be considered rude if I did not stop and introduce myself at the house first. I had not told Catherine I was coming, not wanting her to make a great fuss over my visit.

At the door, I placed my bag on the ground and rubbed my hands together to encourage the circulation. Once the feeling had returned, I knocked on the door frame and waited.

The door opened.

"Good morning," I said. "I'm—"

Then I had no words.

The man in the doorway was about thirty-seven, with blond hair that was going gray at the temples. He leaned lightly on a cane held in his left hand, and his leg on that side seemed not to be entirely straight. He was neatly dressed, clean shaven, and with familiar blue eyes.

It was, unmistakably, Jonathan.

"Ophelia," he said.

"Yes," I said. "Yes, of course. But I don't understand."

I looked at the hand that leaned on the cane. There was a wedding band on his finger.

"You're married," I said.

"To Catherine," he said.

"But you can't be," I said. "You're married to me."

"That was a lifetime ago."

"Your voice," I said. "I had almost forgotten the sound of your voice. I would cry myself to sleep in the dark, trying to recall it. It would come to me in dreams, but I could not remember it when awake. Am I dreaming now?"

"No," he said, and his guilty eyes looked away.

"How?" I asked. "The book. They sent me the book. They said you were buried in a common grave at Spotsylvania."

"The fighting at the Shoe," he said. "Everything got mixed up in the mud and the gore of the trench. I lost the book, and it was found with the corpse of another, whom the federals buried with my name. I was covered in so much carnage, and my uniform was in such tatters, that it was impossible for others to know on which side I had fought, and it was impossible for me to tell them. I was brought here, first. When I had my faculties, I arranged for a message, but it was—"

"Lost."

"Yes, lost," he said. "Before the federals seized

the house, I was removed to a private home in Orange County. It was weeks before I could walk, and months before my health returned. When it did, something had changed in me. My heart had grown cold. I became a wanderer."

He couldn't have been discharged. That record would have been impossible to conceal.

"You deserted."

"Yes."

"That is why you changed your name," I said. "Carter, of course. Your middle name."

"They would have thrown me in prison," he said.

"You were a member of the LaDue Survival Brigade."

"Officially, I was dead. I was just another wounded rebel."

"You deserted your army," I said. "And you deserted me."

"But I did not plan on hurting you," he said.

"I waited for you," I said. "I went through hell trying to get any piece of you that I could, back from the other side. I debased myself and was made a fool and made a fool of others. I held séances every year on the anniversary of your death—on the anniversary of what I thought was your death—and waited for the coded message, which of course never came."

"J'attends ma femme."

I await my wife.

Hearing him utter those words, my knees grew weak and I would have fallen to the ground had not Jonathan caught me in his right arm. He smelled the way I remembered, and that made me want to die upon the spot.

"Did you not love me?"

"I wanted to."

I pushed him away and regained my footing.

"Please," he said. "Don't tell Catherine Ann. It would destroy her."

"And is it so much better that I have been destroyed?" I asked. "I was fourteen years old when I married you, and a widow a year later, and I have spent most of my life begging whatever deity who would listen to allow me to see you just one more time. That's all I asked, was to see you one more time. Oh, the things I have offered in trade for that . . . the kinds of bargains I made."

I stopped.

"This is the price," I said, thinking of Granny Doom. "My sense of myself, built upon a cherished and jealously guarded lie."

I picked up my bag.

"You're a bigamist, Jonathan," I said. "And that's the least of it."

"Please," Jonathan said. "It was so long ago. Can't you forgive me?"

I smiled.

"No," I said. "And I can't forgive myself, either. This wasn't even all that good of a mystery. But the clues were there, all along. All of those desperate séances, with no contact. And Catherine's letter. If only I had read a little more deeply, but I was too distracted by the thought that you could be, somehow, alive."

He smiled sadly.

"But I did survive."

"I did not," I said. "It broke me. And now I'm broken all over again."

I picked up my bag, turned, and walked back up the lane to the Orange Turnpike without once looking back. But I did not cry. My emotions had been stripped as bare as the trees lining the road.

23

Boston was a city built on melancholy. It was the farthest geographical point from my birthplace I had ever been, the farthest north, and the farthest east. The farthest spiritually. The people sounded strange, the buildings were ancient, their customs alien. A freezing rain fell from a sky that was the same color as the harbor.

Old Statehouse Publishers was on Hancock Avenue, within sight of the state capitol. The door was a heavy oak affair, with a knocker in the shape of a pilcrow. Only moments after I tapped the paragraph symbol against the wood, the door swung open.

Garrick Sloane was a kind man of seventy with a fringe of white hair around his pink head and eyes that, behind his spectacles, looked to be 140 years old, and he ushered me inside.

There were books everywhere.

Not only were books overflowing from the desks and shelves, they were piled on the floor and jammed behind doors and perched on windowsills. You could hardly see any of the room behind or between the books. It was as if the books, like rabbits, had multiplied on their own.

Sloane apologized for the state of the office, muttering something about having to take an inventory one of these days, and led me back to an inner room with a fireplace. There was a cheerful Christmas tree in the corner of the room, so crowded by books on the floor that it leaned to one side. Sloane took some books that had been piled on the seats of a pair of chairs, relocated them to the floor, and we sat.

"Aren't you afraid of a fire?" I asked, looking at how near the books were to the hearth. "All it would take is one spark."

"Oh, no," he said, and nudged one of the piles with his foot. "We've never burned a book here, I assure you. Well, we may have scorched a few. But they are really quite safe where they are."

"Of course," I said.

"Ophelia Wylde, Ophelia Wylde," he said. "What a pleasure it is to finally meet my frontier correspondent. I was excited to receive your telegram last week that you would be paying a visit in person. How were your travels? Expensive, I'll wager."

"Dreadfully," I said.

"You mentioned stopping in Virginia on your way," he said. "Was your business successful there?"

"It was conclusive," I said.

"Good, good," he said. "Would you care for

some tea and cake? Just tea, then? Certainly. I'll have Rogers fetch us some. Rogers! Oh, I don't know where the lad has gone. Is that the manuscript I spy beneath your arm?"

I handed over the pages containing the spirit telegraph adventure.

"Ah," he said, thumbing through them. "A bit shorter than the last."

"I was forced to leave some things out," I said.

"What things?" His eyebrows—which were the same shade of yellowing white as the hair on his head—jumped above the rims of his glasses.

"Nothing important," I said.

"But what about your personal code?" he asked. "The agreement will all be revealed to your readers. Are these things that our discerning book-buying public would want to know?"

"The things that are missing are of a personal nature," I said. "Readers would not be interested, I'm sure. The adventure is quite complete without those pages."

He nodded dubiously, then placed the manuscript on a side table. In a few moments a man of somewhat fewer years than Sloane, but even less hair, appeared. Sloane asked for two cups of tea. Rogers grumbled and went away.

"I am pleased to meet you, Mr. Sloane," I said. "I have often wondered what your offices are like, and they are just as I pictured them. This building must be a hundred years old."

"Two hundred, but who's counting?"

That made the building about as old as I felt.

"And you have started on your next?" he asked.

"Next what?"

"Your next adventure," he said. "While we have done a good business over the years in publishing metaphysical texts, your cases of mystic deduction have been a modest success. Just enough to keep publishing them, you understand. So when may we expect your next?"

"I'm unsure."

"What do you mean?

"I'm afraid this may be the final installment."

"Say it is not so, say it is not so."

"It may indeed be so," I said. "This last case has taken something out of me that may be difficult to replace, Mr. Sloane. You have been very kind to me, and I am thankful for all of your help, and it makes me sad to think of disappointing those who would like to follow me on another adventure. But it may be time to give up the ghost."

We sat in silence for a few minutes, and then Rogers brought the tea.

The cup warmed my hands, no books had caught fire, and I was relieved to be just sitting for a moment.

"Tell me, Miss Wylde," Sloane said. "What else would you do?"

"Pardon?"

"If you are no longer pursuing cases and writing about them," he said, "what would you do? Marry? Teach school? Something else?"

"Something else," I said. "A former profession."

Sloane sipped his tea.

"You were a confidence woman."

"Yes."

"A swindler, a cheat, a huxtress, and a hoaxer."

"You know I was."

"You only cheated those who deserved it."

"Oh, we all deserve it, at one time or another," I said. "You know my history. You've edited my books."

Sloane smiled.

"Sounds like a life full of excitement," he said. "Not without its risks, of course, but a life in which one could be richly rewarded for a modicum of effort. But Ophelia—I beg your pardon, but may I address you as such? I have more than a little avuncular feeling for you—there is a problem."

"What, Uncle Sloane, would that be?"

"You cannot undiscover a country."

"Pardon?"

"'*The undiscovered country*,'" Sloane quoted, "'*from whose bourn no traveler returns—it puzzles the will.*'"

"*Hamlet*," I said.

"That's Shakespeare's way of talking about death," Sloane said. "It seems appropriate, in an inverse way, to your circumstance. A precious few human beings are allowed a glimpse of the undiscovered country of the dead; for better or ill, you are among this select lot. You are no charlatan, I am convinced, but the genuine article. How, then, do you resort to a life of fraud? A good confidence woman must first fool herself into believing what she is trying to convince her mark of. How can you do that, having surveyed the terrain? The simple matter is, you cannot. Human experience flows inexorably only in one direction. You, my dear Ophelia, have stood upon that peak in Darien, and related what you have seen—and now here we sit, looking at one another with wild surmise."

I put down my tea.

My first thought was to tell him that he was mixing his literary references, and that Keats had it all wrong, that it wasn't Cortez and his men who stood on that mountaintop in Panama and saw the Pacific, it was Balboa. But I didn't want to argue the point with the old man.

"You are right," I said, finally. "I am denied even a way to make a living."

Sloane leaned forward and placed a gentle hand upon my knee.

"You have suffered something frightful," he said. "Something more than that, I imagine, because you navigate fear uncommonly well. Whatever it is, my dear, the pain will pass. Not all of it, perhaps, and not all at once. But the day will come when you return to yourself, and the world will be right once more, and you will be glad for having not given up the ghost. Now, are you sure I cannot interest you in some cake?"

24

Consider your death, as my inner voice had urged me.

It is the ultimate solution to that most urgent and personal of mysteries, yet who among us—at least those who are not gravely ill or sentenced to death or otherwise facing imminent and inescapable demise—gives it more than a casual thought? The pious tend to reflect not upon death itself but the life that is promised after; the grieving, upon the crushing loss at the death of another; and the wealthy, upon monuments of stone or charity in the vain hope that it may snatch a sliver of immortality from the great destroyer.

What happens to us at the moment of death is as unknown to us as the far side of the moon, yet it is exactly as common a human experience as birth. It is the surest and most democratic thing in the world, immune to wealth, power, beauty, wisdom, or worth. It strikes down the wicked and the just in equal measure. It is as unfeeling and as immutable and as bright and as hard as all jagged things.

Such has been my disposition that, since childhood, I have often remained awake, pondering such impenetrables until dawn smudged the eastern sky. I have never feared death, for I have ample evidence for the survival of the spirit, at least in some form, but probably not in any theology now imagined, not in Summerland or any of the hundred other hymns we whistle while walking past the local burying ground.

The dead talk to us endlessly. Sometimes they come as revenants, appealing to the living in cryptic and dreamlike language for help in squaring some unfinished business before they can cross over. But mostly, the dead speak to us in more prosaic form. Books bring us the essence of those who may be centuries dead, but whose voices remain vibrant through the centuries. Even though I feel my pulse thumping in my wrists as I pen these lines, and hear the scratch of the nib across the paper, and shiver from the night air slipping beneath the window sash—even though I am fully and consciously and gloriously alive as I write—I may be long dead by the time you read these words.

Consider, then, that I speak to you from the grave.

And I will end this tale at, well, the ending, where I began, or very nearly so; because time flows in only one direction, with nary an eddy; because one must complete the journey into uncharted time before it can be mapped; and

because this is my story and it suits my purposes
to do so.

Leaving New England behind, I returned to
the agency in Dodge, but my misery lingered.
The new year came and passed. The chill between Calder and me deepened. I accompanied
McCarty, who seemed to remember little of his
poisoning ordeal, to Boot Hill Cemetery to see
the last of the dead exhumed to make way for
new houses. And then, having grown tired of the
voice in my head that urged self-destruction, I
took the law book down from the shelf beneath
the bust of Lincoln and prepared the papers
necessary to file for divorce in Ford County from
Jonathan Wylde.

I took the pages from my desk that were missing from the manuscript I had left with Sloane
and thoughtfully added some new ones, including the one you read now, and put them in the
post. And by the time you read this—whether
in a few months, or a few years, or a hundred
years—I will have sought out Calder at the Saratoga, interrupted his billiards game, and asked
him to share a late breakfast with me. I imagine
it will be scrambled eggs with ham, or perhaps
bacon.